NANETTE'S CAPTURE

BRACKISH BAY
BOOK 1

CERISE NOBLE

Published by Romance Ink
An Imprint of
ABCD Graphics and Design, Inc.
A Virginia Corporation
977 Seminole Trail #233
Charlottesville, VA 22901

Nanette's Capture
Cerise Noble

eBook ISBN: 978-1-63954-604-6
Print ISBN: 978-1-63954-597-1

DEDICATION

Cruithne

You believed in me, even when I didn't, and better, gave me the tools to make your belief come true.

"SHUSH! SUZANNA, THEY'LL HEAR YOU!"

"I don't care!" My sister swatted at the mosquitoes swarming around her and swore.

I jerked back around, hissing between my teeth. "Dammit, Suzanna, shut up!" Shimmying forward again, I raised the battered binoculars. There they were. The guards to the village. I scanned the top edge of the fence, looking for the name. HodgePodge. Dammit. I slid down, flopping onto my back. Dammit.

"What is it?"

"We're not there yet."

"Why? What is this one?"

"HodgePodge."

My sister wrinkled her nose. "Stupid name."

I agreed. "Stupid name."

"You sure they didn't just rename Caladonia?"

I bit my lip, thinking about it. The weaker villages changed hands frequently, as various warlords took them over. I flipped around onto my belly and shimmied back towards the top of the little crest of land. The palisade didn't look that new. There were some old burn marks here and there, and a few replacement logs, but it didn't look like it had been destroyed and rebuilt, which it would have had to be, if it had been won in a battle. At least, I thought so. I'd never seen a battle up close. But once, on the way here, we'd watched from a far vantage point as a horde swooped in and set fire to everything in reach in the village we were heading to. We'd taken the long way around.

I eyed the towers on the corners. The sentries were all wearing blue and brown. The same colors as the tattered flag flapping in the breeze. "It doesn't look like it."

"Let me see."

I sighed, and handed over the binoculars. Suzanna squirmed forward and looked. After a long moment, in which I had to flick off no less than three creepy crawlies, she slid back down to me. "I guess you're right."

It shouldn't gall me, that my little sister no longer trusted my word or opinion immediately. But it did. She was five years younger – a teenager, all of fourteen, with the know-it-all attitude that came with the age. My mother would have shaken her head and petted my hair, then done the same to Suzanna. *Girls*, she would have said. *You have to trust each other.* I remembered her rings, the ones she said we'd have when we were grown. They matched, just like Suzanna and I did. Was she wearing them when she woke us up to flee? I didn't remember them on her hands, something that would have seemed strange had not the entire morning been strange and awful.

I bit back a whimper. Not knowing what happened to her... it ate a hole in my heart. I took the binoculars back. "We're going to have to take the north side. I don't see a good path around to the south – there's not enough cover."

"Can't we just go in?" Her whining was going to be the death of me, I swear.

"No way. You remember what Daddy said. You have to assume the worst. If you don't know for sure that the people in a village will defend you, don't get near them. Getting trapped inside is a prison sentence, or worse. Fleeing from them, in the depths of the swamp, gives you a chance."

She sighed and rolled her eyes. I'd had many opportunities to repeat Daddy's words since we'd left home. She knew just as well as

I did how dangerous it could be to get captured. My heart ached – I needed my daddy, dammit. He'd know just what to do.

"I'm hungry."

I took a deep breath. No matter how annoying she could be, Suzanna was my responsibility. "Then we're going to have to get far enough away from here. We can't risk them seeing the smoke, you know that."

Typical teenager fashion, Suzanna rolled her eyes, but started crawling down the slope, back to where we'd left our packs. Once there, she hefted hers, and we disappeared into the trees.

Hiking through the forests was difficult, if you didn't know how to walk. If you tried to walk the way you did on a road, you were doomed to fail. Instead, you had to walk near the trees, in a sort of zigzag pattern. If you kept your feet on the roots, or nearby, you ran far less risk of sinking into the bog.

Luckily for Suzanna and me, we'd grown up in the forest. There was a river nearby, and Daddy had fished. So we'd grown up with full stomachs and nimble feet.

It was dark by the time I felt safe enough to stop, the crickets and frogs a cacophony that hid the sound of our steps. We found a stream with a dozen varieties of little fish, and set a small net between two rocks. Suzanna climbed the nearest tree, then returned with a handful of branches and a report.

"I think we're directly north of HodgePodge, maybe slightly to the east. The wind is coming our direction, so I think we're going to be okay with the smoke."

"Thanks." I pulled out the broken branches I'd collected since the last time we'd built a fire, carrying them in a mesh pack so they'd have a better chance of drying before we needed them next. We settled a few rocks in place and built the fire, working together, like we were supposed to, like we had since she was born.

Once the flame took the dry branches and seemed stable enough, I added the green ones Suzanna had collected. They were dryer than ones on the ground level, but they still smoked and flickered. I checked the net. Four little fish – not much for a meal, but better than nothing. I scooped them out, leaving the net in place, and Suzanna and I each cut two open, gutting and cleaning them as quickly as we could. The entrails went in the fire, and the smoke smelled delicious for a moment. My mouth filled with saliva as I remembered my mother cooking the same way. Suzanna had found tubers along the water, and she cleaned them, dicing them with the knife our father made. The water in the pan had boiled, so I tossed in the tubers, and when they were nearly tender, the fish and a handful of edible leaves.

"That smells so good."

I nodded, stirring it a bit more than necessary. "You find any more greens?"

She shook her head, eyes on the pot. It wasn't long before we were scooping it into our bowls, then shoveling it into our mouths. I burned my tongue, but I didn't care.

Too soon, the pot was empty, and I washed it, packing everything away except for the net in the stream. We doused the fire and draped a mosquito net over a branch above us. Curled up next to each other, our blankets kept out the worst of the dampness. As tired as I was, I found myself lying awake, staring at the clouds and listening to the night noises.

"Nanette?"

I shifted, wrapping my arms around my sister. "What?"

"Can you tell me what Daddy said, again?"

I nodded against her hair, the tangles scratchy on my skin. I let myself picture the day, two months ago, that we left our home.

"He woke me up before the sun was up. He said, 'There are people on the way here. Dangerous people, people who will hurt you and your sister if they catch you. You have to wake up. You have to go – now.'"

"And you got up."

"I got up. And Mom had two packs ready to go. She was so angry – that's when I knew it was serious."

"What else did Daddy say?"

"You heard him. Mom woke you up too." She was quiet. "He

said 'Run. Go to Torrent and meet us there. Go to Solon first and ask for John Baker. From there go to Caladonia and ask for Simon Tire. They will help you along the way with supplies and protection. As for Hamel Dirk in Torrent. You can stay with him until we get there.'" I kissed the back of her head. "He said, 'Guard Suzanna with your life. Stay out of sight of everyone. Stay out of villages. Stay away from camps and settlements. Don't trust anyone until they prove you can. Trust your instincts.'"

"They both said 'I love you.'"

"Yes, they did." I paused, taking a deep breath, waiting to see if she would ask.

"And after that?"

"He said 'Mom and I will find you before the year is up. If we don't, we are dead – leave us to the afterlife.'" I bit my lip hard, attempting to still the trembling. "He said, 'Go on, live well, love someone who can protect you. Make me proud.'" I couldn't help it. I always cried. No matter how many times I repeated the words, they still caused tears. In my embrace, my sister cried, too.

Eris. I closed my eyes, seeking the goddess my father used to mention sometimes. Why can't you tell me if they are dead or alive? As usual, there was no reply.

Eventually, we slept.

MORNING WAS BRIGHTER THAN USUAL. THE SUN FOUND US BESIDE THE stream, piercing the green canopy. I rubbed my eyes and sat up, pulling down the mosquito netting and packing it up, then checking the net. There were six fish this time, and I sent a prayer of thanks to the stream for providing. I kicked Suzanna, and she woke with a grumble, but sat up when I indicated the fish. Cleaning them took no longer than it had the night before, but we didn't risk a fire. Tossing the chunks of raw fish into a pottery jar I poured a little vinegar over them, sealed it, and shook. There. They would keep most of the day like that. We each reached in and took a couple chunks, licking our fingers and resealing the jar. I tucked it carefully into the special pouch in my pack. We shook out our blankets before fastening them around our shoulders like cloaks, and we started walking again.

The day passed as all the days had. Slowly. I fingered the date necklace I wore. There were beads of different colors for each month, and beads of the same color for each day in the month. I had a small clip I placed beside the bead for the day, and I moved it now, marking off another day gone. Two and a half months gone now. Seventy-eight days since we'd started to run. I tried not to think about it, but when you're walking through the forest, there's not much to do. You keep an eye out for boggy ground. You keep an ear and an eye out for running water. You keep an ear and an eye out for crocodiles or other predators. You keep an ear and an eye and your gut tuned for humans – the worst predators. You walk. You stay as quiet as you can. And you try not to make yourself into a complete crazy woman with worrying about your family.

We stopped every so often to rest and take another bite of sour fish. It was flakier than raw, but not as flaky as cooked. I checked the sun and tried to keep us walking on the correct path.

"We should have found Caladonia by now." Suzanna was slightly ahead of me, to my right. She spoke without looking at me, so I knew she was scared. Even more so, I was scared.

"Yes, we should have."

"Do you have enough supplies?"

"We'll be fine."

"What about the vinegar? It looked like the jug was pretty light this morning."

"Maybe I'm just getting stronger." There was silence for so long I started to hope she'd accepted my explanation.

"Or maybe you just don't want to tell me you're worried."

The worry burst out of me before I could stop it. "Of course I'm worried! Who wouldn't be? I'm trying to trek across country with a stupid teenager!"

Her face was red and angry when she stopped and planted her feet. "You're a damn teenager, too, you know! Who made you in charge? I just want to know." She started to cry, and then I recognized myself, my hatred of uncertainty. I took a halting step, and then folded her in my arms.

"We're running real low on vinegar. I'm afraid we've passed Caladonia. John told us it would only take a few weeks to reach it, and we've been on the way for forty-one days since we left Solon." Not for the first time I wished I had packed the map properly the last time we'd had to ford one of the bigger streams. Water had damaged it severely, and every time I got it out it was worse – by last week it had been completely useless. "I don't think there's anything we can do except keep going, and try to find Torrent. We have each other. We have equipment. We won't starve to death as long as there's fish in the water, and, like Daddy says, there's always fish in the water." Suzanna shifted, and I could feel her start to smile. "Even if we have to stop more often to fish, if we can't keep it in the vinegar, all it means is that it will take us longer to get there. Not a huge deal." I pushed her back, catching her eyes. "Okay?"

She nodded, taking a deep breath and scrubbing her face with the tattered cuff of her sleeve. "Okay."

Of course, as those who remember Eris know, life has never gone as planned. It was two days later when my life, as I knew it then, ended.

"WATCH OUT." I HELD BACK THE BRAMBLES FOR SUZANNA, PRESSING forward. I could hear the stream; we hadn't eaten since the day before. It was hilly here. It had been too long since we were near enough to water to fish. It was getting late, and we needed to find a place to camp.

"I see it."

The stream turned out to be a river, much larger than I'd thought at first. We rushed to it, grateful for the water and the fish. I unfolded the net and we scouted along the bank, looking for a good spot to set it up. We'd just placed it and started to unpack for the night when I saw it. A small fence made of chain, no higher than a handspan, disappearing into the brush on either side. I hadn't noticed it when we'd crossed it the first time – and it seemed to follow the river, at least in this area. A prickle started along my spine as I stood up, trying to trace its compass with my eyes. I'd never seen anything like it before, but it was man-made. Man made fences – ones that were not completely degraded in the years since the bombardment that nearly destroyed civilization – might mean there were men about. I swung around, scanning the river as far as I could see either direction. There was nothing. But I still couldn't shake the prickle that was telling me something wasn't right. "I think we need to go."

"But I'm starving! I just got the blankets set up. We'll be protected here, under the willow."

I turned again, looking for the edge of the fence, but try as I might I couldn't tell where it crossed the river. It wasn't possible that the entire river was inside it, was it? My belly clenched, and I felt my heart speed up.

"Something is wrong. Suzanna, something is very, very wrong. We need to get out of here. Now!" My voice had risen as unreasoning panic set in, and she paused, then caught sight of my face. She started stuffing everything back in the pack, and heaved it onto her shoulders. I took her hand and we both started to run, back the way we'd come.

"What about the net?" The net! Without that, we'd have a much harder time feeding ourselves.

"Keep going, I'll get it. I'll be right back."

"No!"

I tried to pry her fingers off me, but she held fast, her face white and terrified.

"No! Don't leave me!"

I took a deep breath and we ran back to the net. I snatched it out, folding the frame up and stuffing it in my pack, lone captured flopping fish and all. It would suffocate soon enough. We had just turned to run again when I crashed into a man. Suzanna screamed, and I stumbled back, wildly searching for a way out. Darting to the right, dragging her with me, he moved too quickly and cut off our escape. Encumbered by the packs, we weren't nearly as nimble as we needed to be. I darted to the left, but Suzanna and I collided and went down, a flailing pile of limbs. His hand closed on my arm and dragged me upright.

"You're on our property."

Another man appeared behind him, a weapon of some sort in his hands.

"No!" I panted, holding tight to Suzanna, who knelt on the ground, sobbing. "No! I'm sorry. I'm so sorry. Here – I'll give you back the fish from your river. We'll leave now. No trouble. No trouble at all. I'm sorry." I tried to shake him off, so I could reach the fish in my pack, but his grip didn't budge. I didn't dare let go of Suzanna. "Please sir. I'm so sorry. We're just passing through. We don't want any trouble. We'll leave now." I had avoided his eyes until now, but finally I looked up, hoping my pleas had reached him.

His eyes were hot, and hungry, and somehow I didn't think it was for fish. My stomach dropped. I gasped, then fought hard against his grip. I let go of Suzanna, and tried to pry his fingers off. It didn't do a bit of good. In terror and frustration, I bit him. His flesh was salty sweet, thick in my mouth as I dug my teeth into his forearm. He didn't let go – instead he slapped me with his free hand, hard, hard enough to daze me and I sank down, Suzanna's hysterical screams echoing in my ears.

"You're coming with me."

My begging fell on deaf ears, and I found myself relieved of my pack, which the other man stowed in a boat I hadn't seen, camouflaged in the reeds. The first man took Suzanna's pack, and for a moment we were alone and unbound. I grabbed her hand and jerked her to her feet, and we ran for the bushes we'd come through the first time. He got there first and caught me around the waist, lifting me up while I kicked and beat at his arms with my fists. Suzanna stood frozen, terrified of the man, terrified of being alone.

"Go! Run! I love you!" I screamed at her, willing her to save herself. But would she even survive? Without our equipment, no net, no pot, no blanket... nothing. Would she be able to live, all on her own? She remained rooted to the spot. The man shoved me into the broad bottomed boat, rocking it, then chains were clamped around my wrists and I was caught, face down and bound. I screamed, and his big hand crashed down on my bottom. I shut up, realizing, belatedly, that if we were to be captured, biting and screaming were not the ways to ensure my safety, or that of my sister. The other man stalked towards her, and I rolled onto my side, trying to lever myself up on my elbow to watch. She stood still, petrified, and he scooped her up, tossing her over his shoulder as if she were a feather pillow. He walked back to the river and set her down on the bench in the end of the boat, carefully. Far more gently than I'd been thrown down, and I was grateful.

He spoke to her. "You sit there and behave yourself, and we'll take care of you. Understand?" She nodded, dumb with shock and terror. I worried about the pallor under her tan skin, but I could do nothing about it now.

"Where are you taking us?"

The second man stayed on the shore, and the first sat on the middle bench and started rowing, his massive arms flexing and straightening with each stroke.

"I'm taking you to the governor of this patch of land."

"Please. Just let us go. We'll be on our way, and he'll never know. We mean no harm. We didn't intend to trespass."

"But you did." He paused for a few strokes, regarding me with that intense gaze. "And you bit me. How would I explain that?" I looked then, guilty, as crimson crescents welled on his forearm.

"I'm sorry. I was afraid."

He smiled then, a predatory smile that made my stomach knot itself together. "You should be."

I must have dozed, worn out from fighting. I came to with a start, a horrible crick in my neck from the odd angle I lay in at the base of the boat, and met Suzanna's eyes. They were huge with fear, and my heart dropped to my stomach as I realized she was a virgin. Tommy, the son of the other fisherman nearby, had left with his family before she was old enough to want to experiment. The boy I'd fumbled and played with until we'd learned how sex worked and sated our curiosity on each other.

The boat bumped the dock, and suddenly there were more men around us, shouting and talking. I struggled to sit up. A blindfold was wrapped around my eyes and I panicked, kicking and flailing. Hands were carrying me, and I got a leg loose. Twisting out of their hands, I found myself falling. The splash drove the sound out of my ears and the breath out of my lungs. I clamped my lips shut, struggling futilely with the chain on my wrists as water closed over my head. I could feel the current pushing me, sluggish but steady. With the blindfold on, I couldn't even see which way was up, so I kicked, wiggling like an eel, desperate for air. My lungs burned, and spots danced before my eyes. I considered whether drowning would be better than whatever fate the men had in store for me... and decided I could not give up, not while they still had Suzanna. Hands closed on my arms and I was hauled out of the river. I was dumped on my side, my arm and head thumping the wooden pier. Suzanna was screaming again. Suddenly she was at my side, shaking me and sobbing. I coughed, dragging air into my sandpaper lungs.

"I'm fine," I told her, and she was taken away. I blinked against the wet blindfold, struggling to see who knelt in front of me now.

His voice was deep and he was angry. "Give me one good reason to keep you alive, and not throw you back in for the crocodiles." My heart beat against my ribs, and I snorted the water out of my nose, sneezing and coughing.

"If you weren't sure, why did you pull me out the first time?" I was genuinely curious, hanging on to any thread that would keep me from remembering that I'd just about been a crocodile snack.

"Jeffrey did that." His voice turned into a growl. "Against

orders." Jeffrey? I wondered if that was the man who'd captured me. And why would he do such a thing?

"What do you want with me?"

He guffawed. "Too stupid to know she's not the one who should be asking questions." He stood up. His heavy tread moved away from me, down the pier.

A woman's voice next. "Well, she's here now. Put her in the dungeon."

Big hands dragged me up while others removed my boots. I started to babble. "My sister. She's only twelve. Please. Don't hurt her. Please. I'll do whatever you say."

There was a pause in the movement around me, and the woman's voice again. It was softer. "We won't harm the child. Take her to the kitchen."

My sister's voice. "No! I don't want to leave her!"

I swung my head towards her voice, and put as much authority in it as I could muster. "Suzanna. Go. I am fine. I am a grown woman. You are a child. Do you understand?"

The was a hitch in her sobbing as she realized a little of what I'd said. I prayed she didn't understand all of it, only the part that meant she was safe. I was starting to grasp some of the shape of their honor. They wouldn't rape a child. Me, on the other hand?

A shaky breath. "Yes. I understand."

There were footsteps, big heavy ones and little stumbling ones. A few of the iron bands on my chest loosened and I took as deep a breath as I could manage. The hands on my body dragged me forward, and I went as willingly as I could. Survival meant pleasing my captors – being useful. And as long as they took care of Suzanna, as long as they didn't harm her, I would do my best to be pleasing and useful.

The dungeon was surprisingly dank and chilly. I was shoved in, and I stumbled, scraping my knees on the concrete ground as I fell, unable to balance with my hands chained behind my back. The door made a final clunking sound as it closed. I sank down, and gave into the fear. Hot tears dampened my blindfold, and my chest shook with sobs. Eventually, I slept.

WHEN I AWOKE, IT WAS MORNING. OR AT LEAST, IT SEEMED LIGHTER beyond my blindfold. It felt like morning. I realized I must have lost my date necklace to the river, and I spent a moment missing it. Then I stretched as best as I could, my wrists still bound, my joints hurting from a night on an unforgiving surface. Standing up, I nearly lost my balance to lightheadedness, but deep breaths gave me enough strength to straighten. I slid a foot out tentatively, then, when it touched nothing but floor, shuffled forward. Again. Again. I continued until abruptly I stubbed my toe on the far wall, and bit back a cry. Leaning my head forward, I pressed my forehead to the wall and then turned, leaning on it with my right arm. I started to shuffle forward again, determined to learn the shape of my prison, when I ran into something. It was large, and hard, and the smooth planes spoke to me of durability and long use. The further I explored it with my cheek, the more it frightened me. Chains clanked against it, and I shivered. They had called this a dungeon. I wondered if this was a torture device. The door opened behind me, and I jerked away, bumping my head on the wall and startling a cry from me.

It was the woman's voice again. "We're going to get you cleaned up."

I swallowed, uncertain, and I heard her soft footsteps coming towards me.

"Normally, we take the people we catch in our territory to the village and sell them. But Jeffery seems to have taken an interest in you. He's asked the governor if he can keep you." I nodded, not sure which was the more horrifying fate. "We'll keep your sister – Suzanna, is it? It's not safe for a girl to wander around alone. We won't harm her. She'll have to work for her keep, of course. But she'll be treated as a daughter, a precious child." Her finger slid along my grimy face and I flinched back. "Being sold is an uncertain fate. Roy tries to vet the people he sells to – but nothing is certain in this day and age. It is not impossible to fool him, just very difficult." Four fingertips slid along my face now, caressing my jaw line. I flinched again. "Did he hit you?" I nodded, a hot, shameful feeling in my belly. "I saw the bite on his arm. I'd say you got off lightly."

I didn't want to be sold – not if it meant I might never see Suzanna again, would be leaving her in the hands of people I didn't know and didn't trust. "Please." I swallowed hard, my throat dry, and tried again. "Please. I'll be good. I'll please Jeffery."

She laughed a little. "I dare say he'll be pleased enough for the opportunity to teach you not to bite people bigger and stronger than you." A cold chill washed over my skin and I shuddered. She tapped my face. "I'll tell Roy you'll be worth keeping." I nodded, relieved and afraid at the same time.

Her footsteps, and then the door closed. I sagged against the wall, shivering violently. Sinking to my knees, I waited. The door opened again, and I heard masculine grunts. Then the sound of something being set down, and a splash of water. The woman's voice again. "It's warm enough." Suddenly there were big hands on my arms, hauling me forward. I was placed beside what felt like a huge wooden tub. I could feel the steam rising, and suddenly that seemed like the most glorious, luxurious thing in the world. I'd had nothing but quick dips in the occasional stream since leaving home, and my body ached. My blindfold was taken off, and I blinked, blinded in the sudden light. When I was able to focus again I saw a woman, taller than myself, with a perfect, slim hourglass figure and long black hair. She wore a chain around her slender throat, but given her bearing I wasn't sure if it was a sign of high or low status. A richly colored red linen dress fell gracefully from her shoulders, leaving her arms bare, with another chain wrapped around her waist. She smiled, and the temperature in the room dropped another few degrees. I shivered, and her smile widened. "Strip her."

Suddenly, I remembered the two men beside me. I flinched, but made no move to resist as the first man tore my shirt from neckline to wrist. A tear slipped out, and I tried to stop remembering my mother sewing it. It was tattered and mud stained by our long travel, practically rags. I can do without it, I told myself sternly. The other man tore my pants off, leaving just my breast binding. I panted, trying not to panic. The man to my left produced a small knife and slid the flat side against my skin, cutting through the bindings that held my breasts as flat as possible to my chest. The cloth fell away, my heavy breasts bouncing in the air. I stood nude before them, grimy from travel, despite my dunk in their river. I glanced at the man on my right and recognized my captor from the heat in his eyes. My nipples hardened under his gaze and I shrank back, afraid of what he would do.

"Jeffery?" Her voice was not sharp, it was almost deferential. "Wouldn't you prefer her to bathe, first?" So it was Jeffery. The man who wanted to keep me. Despite myself, I found a welling gratitude that his lust was allowing me to stay with my sister. Eris. I called to the goddess in my head, but, as usual, she didn't answer. Please help me be good enough to protect Suzanna.

"Yes."

The black-haired woman pointed to a chamber pot to the side. "Piss, first." I flushed red, not wanting to relieve myself in front of all of them, but I wasn't being given a choice. Humiliated, I squatted, keeping my eyes on the ground, and pissed into the pot. One of the men took it away, and the woman gestured at the tub, so I stepped in, sinking into the warm water with a sigh. It was softened with some sort of scented oil, and I inhaled, willing myself to relax against the side of the tub.

Jeffery's eyes never left me, and I felt prickles of awareness follow his gaze as it trailed over my shoulders, then lower. "Stephanie."

"Yes, sir?" So she was lower rank. Good to know.

"Leave." She pouted, momentarily put out, until he gave her a sharp warning glance. Then she turned on her heel in a huff and practically stormed out. I wondered what had angered her. I glanced up when the other man returned. He stood watching me with a half-smile. It was then that I realized the men were related.

They had the same shape of nose with a broad base and upturned tip. I almost smiled before I caught myself and bit my lip. When I was able to look at them without immediate terror, they were actually quite attractive. Tall, muscular, with the broad shoulders and slim hips that seemed built for power. They both wore sleeveless shirts, with chains around their thick necks, a round medallion hanging from each one. Overalls made of some sort of canvas material covered them from mid chest to ankle, and their feet were bare. Jeffery knelt beside the tub, a rough cloth in his hand. He dipped it in the water and, his eyes boring into my own, lifted it dripping to scrub my shoulder. I flinched at the touch, and then relaxed. He wasn't harming me. It was scratchy, but it didn't really hurt.

I dropped my eyes under the intensity of his. He continued to wash me, scrubbing my neck to the tops of my breasts. His big hand closed in my hair and held my face still. "Close your eyes." I obeyed, and he scrubbed my face, careful not to get water in my nose. My body awakened under his touch. This might be all the foreplay I was going to get – might as well make the best of it. I allowed myself to lean into his hand. His fingers were thorough, and not exactly gentle, but I found it wasn't as distasteful as I'd originally thought it would be. Stephanie seemed to enjoy quite a few liberties for one who answered Jeffery with 'yes, sir'. Maybe I could earn a few liberties for myself. For now, however... relaxing and allowing my body to feel pleasure where it could, would ease the damage that could be done otherwise.

His hands on my scalp further relaxed me, scrubbing and massaging the scented oil into my short, tangled hair. He pulled me forward, up onto my knees, and the other man unlocked the chain on my wrists. I lifted my arms slowly, and rolled my shoulders, trying to work out the stiffness. Jeffery scrubbed under my arms then, and all the way down to my wrists. Carefully scrubbing each finger, he used his big nail to clean under my little ones. I remained kneeling, closer to him, and caught the scent of his body. It was a clean scent, similar to the oil in my own bath but a little different. It called to me, made me think of autumn, when the temperatures dropped just enough for strong breezes to sweep through the forest and my mother baked with more spices.

His hands scrubbing my breasts brought me crashing back to the present. I gasped as the rough cloth scraped over my hard nipples, crinkling them tighter. He seemed fascinated by their sway and bounce, spending far more time than necessary scrubbing them. I felt my face heat up. I knew big breasts were not useful when working – they got in the way, they flopped around – but they were even more mortifying now. Over and over he went, circling my pink nipples as I hung my head and watched. The shiver started in my spine, but when it finished, my vulva was tingling. I remembered the feeling of ripening from my play with Tommy, and blushed hotter.

His voice was hoarse. "Stand up."

I obeyed, and the other man pulled my legs to the edges of the tub, spreading my thighs until I gasped. Jeffrey scrubbed my belly, my back, then my hips. Skirting the center of my heat, he scrubbed my thighs, then my knees, gentle on my scrapes. Scrubbing down my legs, he lifted a foot to carefully scrub every bit of it, even between my toes. I swayed, and the other man held me steady. I giggled involuntarily as the cloth tickled my foot. He shifted to the other, and then set it down too. Swirling the cloth in the water, he lifted it to scrub between my legs. I flinched, the sensitive flesh there swelling with his attentions. He shifted back, scrubbing my buttocks and between them, until he was satisfied I was as clean as I could be. Mortified by the intimate attention, I squirmed, staying still only when the man holding me made a warning sound in his throat. Jeffery dropped the cloth, and then I felt his bare fingers against my nether lips. I gasped, and he slid them along my slit, not hurting me. I took a deep breath. Time to get ready. I willed myself to relax, to accept what he did. Gently, parting the wet hair, he slipped a finger inside my slit, sliding it up to the nub that sent sparks of pleasure through my body. I gasped again, and he slid it back, finding the deep wet hole he wanted. I grunted when the finger slid inside me. He looked up at the other man and grinned.

"Not a virgin."

I grunted again, his finger inspiring a need that hadn't awakened in a long time. He spread my lips with his other hand, and I flushed redder than Stephanie's dress at the way he watched me there so intently. Slipping his finger in and out, pressing along my inner walls until I squirmed, his eyes never left my vulva.

"Please." I spoke before I realized it, my body taking over my tongue.

He looked up. "Am I hurting you?"

Mute, I shook my head, mortified that so far, it was less like rape and more like the explorations I'd engaged in with Tommy. I suddenly wondered if he wanted it to hurt. He slid another finger in and I gasped, my hips rocking forward and pleasure twisting through my insides.

"Do you want me to?" His question sent a spike of fear through my belly, but instead of drying my arousal it increased it. His fingers became rougher, jamming into me with each word. "Because I can. I want to hurt you, Nanette."

I clung to his shoulders, unsure when I'd grabbed him, and stared into his eyes as he slammed his thick fingers inside me. The man behind me held me, steadying me, supporting me as my knees turned to jelly. One hand was wrapped firmly around my waist, and the other reached up, squeezing and massaging my breasts. My head fell back and then forward again and I panted, groaning with each thrust. When the orgasm hit me I was surprised, crying out in a breathy shriek. Sparks of pleasure swirled through my body and I clenched hard around his fingers. He didn't let up, instead thrust harder until I was wrung out, boneless and shaking. The other man lowered me gently back into the tub. I collapsed against the side and attempted to catch my breath.

Jeffery's hand caressed my cheek. I leaned into it, grateful and content. If serving him involved this kind of pleasure every time, it was a more than fair bargain. I ventured a smile, but his face was stern.

My voice wavered. "Thank you?"

The edge of his lip twitched and I watched him bite back a smile. His voice was gentle, but the underlying steel in the words was not. "I still owe you a spanking for that bite yesterday. And for nearly drowning yourself."

A tingle of fear started in my spine, and my smile wavered. "Spanking?"

"Spanking." He nodded, affirming it. "That's what happens when girls who belong to us misbehave."

I swallowed hard, my eyes darting to his broad, calloused hands. "I'm so sorry. I'll be good."

He actually smiled this time. "I know you will. Especially after your spanking."

CHAPTER
TWO

FEAR SPREAD THROUGH MY LIMBS, but it was having difficulty fighting the lethargy that the pleasure had left behind. He caught me by the hair and I found myself lifted to standing. He tugged, and I stepped out of the tub. For the first time, I noticed our surroundings. All manner of strange unrecognizable furniture lined the walls, most of them dripping with chains. Here and there were benches, and it was to one of these that he led me. Seating himself, I found myself bending to the side to relieve the ache in my scalp. My nipples felt like pebbles in the cool air, and the water running down my thighs mixed with my juices. I shivered.

The other man spoke up. "Do you want a towel for her?"

Jeffery snorted. "Wet skin stings more." I shivered harder, my buttocks prickling in anticipation. He pulled me over his lap, the rough canvas of his overalls scraping my belly and the underside of my breasts.

"Please, sir. I'll be so good. I promise."

His hand slid down the curve of my bottom, and I flinched. His voice was low and soothing. "Yes you will. Well spanked girls are good girls."

Dread settled into the pit of my stomach. My hands fidgeted on the rough concrete floor, and he stroked my wet hair, his fingers trailing along my spine to the top of my crease. His hand left my skin, and I tensed, anticipating the blow. When it fell, it was so much harder than I expected. My breath exploded out of my body with a cry. I suddenly realized just how gentle my father had been when Suzanna and I were spanked at home. The thought of losing my daddy combined with the pain, and I burst into tears.

It didn't deter him. His hand rose again and crashed into my bottom. I sucked in breath, but it didn't help. My bottom was burning, stinging furiously and every spank just amplified the pain. Loud cracks echoed around the room, driving me to distraction. I struggled, but I found my hands pinned to the small of my back, my head dangling helplessly. I kicked until he tucked my legs under his, and then I just lay there, precariously folded over one knee, my tender bottom pinned and exposed for his punishment. I sobbed until snot dripped out my nose, my chest heaving with each shaky breath.

Jeffery stopped, and I tried to stop crying. "Next time I give you an order, you obey it. Without hesitation, without question. Without biting me, and without throwing yourself into the river." I nodded, desperate for the pain to stop. My bottom was on fire, surely I would be bruised for days. He slapped me sharply on the thigh, reminding me he couldn't see a nod.

"The correct answer is, 'yes, sir'."

I nodded again, frantic. "Yes, sir! Yes, sir! I understand! I'll be good, I swear..." My voice trailed off in sobbing. He resumed my spanking, concentrating on my sweet spot and thighs now. I struggled against his hold, but it was unbreakable. His hand covered the width of my thigh in one spank, and I started hiccupping, choking on snot and tears as his fingers branded me. "Please..." Incoherent, I begged.

The other man spoke up. "Jeffery. I think she's learned her lesson."

Jeffery paused, stroking my throbbing bottom. "Have you?" he demanded, slapping my bottom so very hard. "Have you learned your lesson?" Another slap to emphasize the question.

"Yes sir, yes sir, yes sir..."

"All right." He put me on his lap and tucked me against his chest. The rough canvas chafed my raw bottom. His arms held me firmly, but not painfully. So I gave in, too exhausted and too chastened to struggle any more. He drew a handkerchief from his pocket and handed it to me.

He patted my hair until I finally stopped sobbing, wiping my face with the faded gray cloth. His chest was warm and solid against my cheek, and for some unknown reason his scent comforted me. I lay still, my head tucked against the crook of his neck.

I startled when I heard the door open, but it was just the other man exiting. Unreasoning fear rose in my belly – he'd been the one who'd suggested Jeffery stop my spanking. Would he start again, with the other man gone? My fear proved to be unfounded, however, as Jeffery soothed me, stroking my back and patting me until I relaxed against him.

When we had been alone for a time, he spoke. I tried to raise my head to look at his face, but he tucked me back against his shoulder. I complied, feeling the rumble of his voice vibrate. "You belong to me, Nanette. You belong first to Roy, our governor, but I'm sure he'll let me keep you. So you belong to me. I will protect you, and cherish you, and give you pleasure, but in return, I require absolute obedience. Obedience to me, to Roy, and to anyone else he sets above you. Do you understand?"

I nodded, remembering the question about throwing me back to the crocodiles. I would have to learn to be very obedient. His sharp slap to my thigh reminded me that I hadn't quite mastered even the basics yet. "Yes, sir! I understand."

"Good girl."

My breath caught, just a moment, at the unanticipated praise. He continued to stroke my back. "Devon will be back with a clean tub. You'll take just a dip, and then I'll show you where you'll stay." Right on cue, the door opened and the other man returned, lugging another tub with the aid of a man I hadn't seen before. They set it down.

The second man came towards us and caught my chin, examining my face. I blushed, closing my eyes under his scrutiny. "Stephanie was right. You are beautiful. May I?"

Jeffery released me, and I stood on wobbling legs, following the direction of the hand on my chin. He walked partially around me and whistled, running a hand over my aching bottom. It felt cool in contrast to the heat radiating off my skin. "Not nearly as much as Stephanie gets, but then, she's a brat."

I shivered. Stephanie was spanked more severely? And she seemed to have such liberties... my heart sank. I wasn't sure what I'd be allowed to do. So I clung tight to the one thing I did know – for now, for as long as I pleased them enough to not sell me, I was in the same place Suzanna was.

"Probably plenty for this girl, right, girl?"

I nodded quickly. "Yes, sir."

He grinned, genuinely pleased. "A quick learner to boot. You've found yourself a good one, I think."

Jeffrey tugged me back down to his thigh and I squeaked at the flare of discomfort. "I think so."

They left with the dirty water. Jeffery lifted me easily, then deposited me in the fresh tub. The water felt warm and comforting on every part of me except one, and I shifted to my knees to keep my bottom from touching the hard surface. He noticed and reached into the water, squeezing my buttocks until I gasped, fresh tears leaking. When I was rinsed to his satisfaction, he lifted me out and wrapped me in a towel. The rough material sensitized my already oversensitive skin and I whimpered. Tucking me down on my knees, facing away from him, he took a comb and untangled the snarls until my hair was smooth. Somehow, the domestic gesture calmed me. He stood me up, taking the towel away to lie on the handle of the tub. The door opened again and Stephanie entered, her mouth set in an angry line. I flinched away from her blue eyes and Jeffrey wrapped his arms around me.

"Behave yourself."

She humphed, and his voice sharped. "I mean it. I'll tell Tobin."

She narrowed her eyes, but did not answer, instead laying out the clothes that she'd brought. The dress was the same as hers, except blue instead of red, and I realized it was actually not a dress. It was just two strips of cloth, each more than the width of my body and nearly double my height. Each one was knotted in the middle. The knots were placed on my shoulders, the rest was draped around my body, two strips covering my back, and two strips covering my front, held in place by a chain Stephanie clipped around my waist. I gritted my teeth, determined not to whimper when the cloth brushed my tender bottom, but that wasn't good enough for her. She raked her nails across both cheeks and I squealed, jerking away from her. Jeffery caught me, his face dark with anger. He reached for her, but she skipped out of reach, laughing.

Jeffery caught her eye and raised his voice. "Tobin! Your bitch is in need of some discipline."

The color drained from her face and she hissed at him. "It's my right to teach the new girl her place."

Jeffery's retort was sharp. "She knows her place. She just learned it over my knee. She was offering you no challenge."

I cowered against his chest, realizing that Stephanie was far the more dangerous than I'd originally thought.

Tobin appeared in the doorway. She dropped to her knees, felled by the look on his face. He pointed to the floor at his feet, and she crawled to him. Once there, she knelt up, her whole body pleading with him. I couldn't hear if she spoke, but it wouldn't have mattered. His voice was cold and dismissive. "Room. Corner. Now." She stood, throwing him one more pleading look, but he ignored her. She fled.

Jeffery glared at Tobin. "It's a good thing Nanette already had the clothes on, or Stephanie could have cut her." He lifted the fabric away from my bottom, showing Tobin the cat scratches smarting on my skin.

Tobin leaned down for a closer look, frowning. He spoke to Jeffery. "I'll deal with her." Then he turned to me. "You don't have to worry about retribution from her. She knows better."

24

I nodded, but I didn't believe him. He left.

"Come." Jeffery led me out of the bizarre room and into a hall with flat reed flooring that felt warmer and smoother on my bare feet. Many doors opened into this hallway, and I wondered what they were all for. We passed a staircase to the left, and then there was a large opening, the width of four doors, to our right. Inside was a big room with a big table and many chairs, and beyond that was a room that had to be the kitchen. A half wall separated the kitchen from the dining room, and you could see into it that there were two wood burning stoves against the far wall, a sink to one side, and a stout woman in the middle of it. Brandishing a wooden spoon, she dished out a sort of porridge or mash into bowls, tossing in handfuls of chopped fruit and nuts.

"Jacqueline, make sure that doesn't burn!"

"Yes, ma'am." The woman in question stirred a big pot on the stove. She wore a similar dress to mine and Stephanie's, but green in color. Darting between the table and the top of the half wall where the stout woman placed the finished bowls was none other than my little sister. She wore a tunic dress, linen with long sleeves, closed and covering her body completely down to her ankles.

I tried to break away from Jeffery, but he held me tucked against his side. "Suzanna!"

She saw me and set the bowl on the table hastily before launching herself at me. Her arms wrapped tight around me and she trembled. "I was so scared. I heard crying this morning. That wasn't you, was it?"

I patted her hair, smelling the same scented oil that had been in my bath. All was right with the world if she was okay. So I lied. "No, it wasn't me. How about you, are you okay?"

She nodded, her head on my shoulder. She didn't seem to care about the thick arm between us, holding my waist tight.

"They gave me a bath last night. And supper. And a comb. And clothes. And a bed. They have feather beds, did you know that?" She looked up, her eyes filled with concern, so I nodded, as if I'd slept on one too. She put her head back down, reassured. "But they woke me up at the crack of dawn to chop vegetables and fruit and stuff."

She stifled a yawn and I smiled. "You're doing so well. Thank you for helping out."

She peered at my face. "What's your job going to be?"

I glanced at Jeffery, unsure. "I don't know. I think I'm going to find out soon."

He nodded.

She finally focused on him, and skipped back a few steps in alarm. "Nanette, that's the man who caught you!"

I nodded. "I know. But it's okay. He was just trying to protect us." She stared at him, doubtful, taking in the possessive arm around my waist and my new clothing.

"He didn't hurt you, did he Nanette?"

I bit the inside of my lip. How to answer? "A little bit."

"When he slapped you, and when he dropped you in the boat."

I nodded. "Yes."

"This morning?"

"A little bit."

"It *was* you crying! Nanette, please don't, don't do this for me!"

I reached for her, gathering her to me and shushing her. I had to soothe her fear quickly, or she might do something stupid that would get her hurt. I whispered in her ear, quiet and urgent. "He gave me a spanking. You remember, how Daddy spanked us when we fought with each other or did something stupid?"

"But!"

"Remember how you used to holler and kick up a fuss even when it didn't hurt that bad, just so he'd feel sorry for you and stop?"

"Oh!"

I pulled away from her and winked. She bit her lip, uncertain, her eyes darting from me to Jeffrey.

"Besides. You're forgetting. He saved my life."

"You only wiggled because he hurt you to start with." Her lip stuck out mutinously and her hip cocked, a perfect picture of a

26

doubting teenager, loyal to the core. My heart wanted to burst, and I knew then that it didn't matter how many spankings I got, or how annoying she could be. If she was safe, it was worth it.

"True. But he did save me from drowning. For that, I'm grateful."

She sighed and glared at him, but she wasn't protesting any more.

The stout woman from the kitchen chose that moment to recapture my sister's attention. "Suzanna! Enough time wasting, get those bowls on the table!" I focused on her as my sister blanched and darted for the line of bowls on the counter.

Jeffrey took me into the kitchen. "Lauren, this is Nanette."

"So? I'm busy. Get out of my way."

Jeffery stepped back as she grabbed another jar of nuts from the shelves covering one whole wall of the kitchen and tossed a handful on the counter, chopping them quicker than I could count them. "Last one, Suzanna. Then get back in here."

My sister returned and stood waiting for orders. Lauren gestured at the far corner where a stool was tucked. "Corner." She went to it and sat down, watching the room. Lauren took the pot of porridge from Jacqueline, scraping the last of it out into the largest bowl on the counter. I saw four there, one covered in chopped nuts and fruit, and the others plain.

"What do you like on your porridge?"

I wasn't sure whom the question was directed at, so I remained quiet. She looked up, handing the pot to Jacqueline to wash, and focused on me. Her eyes were a startling shade of green. "You, girl. What do you like on your porridge?"

"Anything is fine, ma'am."

"I have raisins. Currants, raspberries, apples, pears and blueberries. Pecans, walnuts and almonds. Dates. Carob. Carrots, onions and beets."

"Um. Raspberries and carob, if you please."

"Coming up." She turned to my sister in the corner. "Girl! What do you want on your porridge?"

"Pears and almonds, please, ma'am."

Lauren finished two of the smaller bowls, then tossed a heaping handful of a fruit mix onto the larger bowl, followed by a handful of mixed nuts. She handed one to me, one to Jacqueline, who had finished washing the pot and hung it up to dry. Then she snapped her fingers and my sister, who'd never been very obedient to start with, sprang up and trotted to her. Lauren handed her a bowl and pointed at a small table near the stool. "Eat."

Suzanna picked up her bowl, then glanced at the man still standing in the kitchen with me.

"Shoo," the large woman said to Jeffery. "The governor will be down soon, and you can get it settled then. Until then, out!"

He frowned at her, but left the kitchen, leaving me standing there with a bowl of porridge in my hands. It was hot and smelled strangely. I took another sniff. The raspberries and carob would be lovely, but I didn't recognize the porridge.

"It's rice."

I looked up.

"Wild and domesticated. Whatever they can harvest now."

"Oh. I... don't think I've eaten it before."

"Really? It's very popular here. Ever since the bombardment on the icecaps turned the planet to swamp, a lot more places can grow rice than before. This blend is very good. I've been getting it from the village nearby. Some of the best rice blenders in the business." She took a bite, savoring it a moment before waving her spoon to emphasize the point. "And I would know. I've cooked in most of the big villages from here to the west coast."

I stared at her in awe. She had traveled across the whole of what used to be the United States of America? Before the – no one could agree if it was war, or terrorism, or a science experiment gone wrong, but they could all agree it was something that catastrophically leveled a few mountains into the ocean and melted the ice caps – bombardment, most people called it. They were probably right. All of the major cities were gone. Some were victims of the bombardment itself. Some were victims of the flooding and the tsunamis. So all the people who used to run the governments were gone. Most people didn't know – couldn't know – what had really happened. Some kind of wave had knocked out all the fancy machinery, also. It was still around. Some of the old people had parents that had remembered how to use it, how to harness the lightning. It was just amusements now – no one had the resources to build another power plant, to put lines in – and what lines were still in existence weren't safe, or so they said. Too much water, too many cut ends where people scavenged the copper. The lightning would skip across the water at every break in the wire, and kill everything it touched. Too risky. But I didn't worry about it. Learning to fish, learning to survive in this world as a girl was difficult enough without worrying about lights that could burn without flame or magic boxes that showed stories.

Still, it gave me a greater appreciation for the solid woman in front of me. She was more muscular than fat, and her gray hair was cropped close to her head. She wore a shirt similar to the top of my sister's dress, but looser around the shoulders, and a pair of overalls like the men. She looked like she was tough enough to take a hike across the continent, a continent where it was no longer safe to be a woman alone.

"Alone?"

"Of course I did it alone. No one else wanted to be that foolish."

I gaped, impressed. She caught my look and raised an eyebrow. I looked down, embarrassed to be caught staring.

"Eat while it's warm."

She pulled out a chair, and I hesitated, glancing at Suzanna. Of course, she was watching me. "Thank you." I sat down, trying to keep from wincing. My bottom throbbed, aching so badly I wanted to jump up and down, but I dared not. So I sat and took a bite. The porridge was far better than I expected. Suddenly, my fatigue and hunger caught up with me, and I shoveled it in my mouth as quickly as I could politely do - politely being a relative term. My sister ate demurely two chairs down, so she must have been fed well the night before. I was grateful.

My stomach comfortably stretched, I examined the only other woman at the table, Jacqueline. She had dark circles under her eyes and short dark curly hair. She ate slowly, as if it were a chore. Lauren nudged her, and she picked up the pace a little, but eventually it slowed back down to a crawl.

"Come on, Jackie. You have to eat. You have to keep up your strength, or you'll go with her."

"I wish I could." Her voice was as hollow as her eyes.

"Don't say that, sweetheart. You aren't going with her. You're staying right here. He'll need you, after, you know."

"I don't care."

That was apparently the wrong answer, because Lauren's voice sharpened. "Your lady does care. She needs to know that you'll stay here, that you'll help him."

"Okay." The acquiescence, said in the same flat voice as the defiance was creepy, and I wondered.

CHAPTER
THREE

THERE WERE a lot of men in the dining room. Lauren seemed to notice my curiosity, and when I craned my neck, trying to see over the half wall, she nodded at me. I stood, cautious, but she didn't gainsay it. So I drifted to the side of the opening where I could look without being too obvious.

There was Jeffery and Devon. I blushed at the reminder of his rough fingers on my skin, and my nipples hardened again. There was Tobin – where was Stephanie? oh. She was kneeling on a cushion at his feet, under the table, humiliation plainly written on her refined face. I felt a tiny glimmer of self-righteous satisfaction before I remembered that I could just as easily find myself in the same position. Which I'd rather not – I didn't want to alarm Suzanna. There was a big man at the end of the table. He ate sparingly, with mechanical motions, as if he derived no enjoyment from the food at all despite it being piled high with fruit and nuts. Most of which was left in the bowl untouched. There was another man near Tobin who I hadn't seen before. All of them wore similar clothing – sleeveless shirts and overalls, a chain on their necks with a medallion. The big man's was slightly larger than the rest. Given that and his position at the head of the table led me to believe that he must be Roy, the governor of this little territory.

Did they not have any other women? I glanced back at the kitchen table. Jacqueline seemed to belong to someone, but I wasn't sure who. Stephanie obviously belonged to Tobin. I was going to belong to Jeffery. But the rest of the men didn't seem to have women. I wondered at that, wondered especially at Roy's lack of a woman. It seemed he would have gotten one before the others – unless the other women they'd caught on their property were unsuitable? And Stephanie seemed to be a lot of trouble. I wondered why they had kept her. I resolved to be well behaved, if only to save my aching bottom from another round with Jeffery's solid hand. Unthinking, I reached back and rubbed, then caught myself and snatched my hand away guiltily. Suzanna didn't seem to have seen, but Lauren gave me an amused look. I colored under her gaze.

Not wanting to sit back down, I continued watching as the men ate, talking quietly among themselves of the various chores. Fishing, mending nets, maintaining the boats and the little fence that marked their territory, the various trip wires and signals they had devised to alert them to anyone crossing it. I learned that there were more men, not just the ones who'd stayed on the other side of the river. It sounded almost like there were multiple camps surrounding this one, and the thought gave me pause. Running away wouldn't have been especially smart on any day, but if there were as many men under Roy's command as there seemed to be, it would be downright impossible.

Roy didn't participate in the conversation, which I found unusual, given that he was their leader. When they had all finished, Tobin nudged Stephanie, and she stood, collecting their bowls and taking them to the counter. I lowered my eyes, but she didn't speak to me. When she returned to her cushion, I took the empty bowls to the sink, and began washing them before I was asked, determined to show myself to be useful.

I was too far away then to hear the subsequent conversation over the sounds of my scrubbing. Jeffery's touch on my shoulder startled me.

"Oh!"

He took my wrist and led me out to the dining room, to Roy's left, before pushing me down to my knees. Roy stared at me for a long moment.

"She looks strong enough to be useful." His voice told me he was the same man who'd threatened to give me back to the crocodiles, and I shivered.

Jeffery answered. "Yes, she is."

"And we have taken her sister into our protection."

"Yes."

"You find her pleasing?"

"I do."

"So you wish to keep her?"

"Yes, sir."

He nodded. "You may keep her. Nanette." He snapped his fingers, and I shuffled forward on my knees. He leaned down, laying a thick chain around my neck and locking it with a small padlock. It seemed that he must have many of these little locks, as the ring on his belt contained many little keys, each with a number engraved on them. "You belong to me, to the House of Brackish Bay. I expect you to obey every command I give you, immediately and without complaint."

"Yes, sir." I bowed my head. I would do almost anything in the world to stay close to my sister, to protect her.

"As Jeffery is a loyal member of my house, I give you to him for his pleasure and use. I expect you to please him well if you wish to maintain the status his ownership gives you."

His ownership gave me status? I wondered what I would be if I was not owned by Jeffery, what had happened to other women who didn't please these men. Were they given to the others, the men who were lower in the ranks, or merely sold? I swallowed hard. "Yes, sir."

"Take her."

Jeffery nodded, and snapped his fingers. I crawled to him, and he stroked my hair, as if I were an animal, a pet. I flushed red. Then he turned and left the room. I looked to Roy, and he dismissed me with a flick of his fingers. I hurried after Jeffrey, afraid to stand, afraid to ask where he was going or what he was doing.

I found myself in the long hall again, and then Jeffery disappeared through one of the many doors. I followed as quickly as I could, finding the door open still. I trembled. He turned to me, and beckoned me in.

There was a rug on the reed floor, softening the impact on my knees, and I knelt in front of his feet where he sat on the bed, gazing down at me with the heat I'd seen before. I blushed, and the fabric over my chest scraped my puckered nipples. I could see the bite on his arm had been cleaned, and it was scabbed over already. He unfastened his overalls, pulling them down to expose his penis. I swallowed hard, eying it. Somehow I didn't remember Tommy's being quite that thick or long. It stood out straight from his body, the thatch of brown hair curling around its base, and a pearly bead of arousal oozing from its tip.

"Please me."

For a moment I wasn't sure what he wanted. And then he ran his fingers through my hair, tightening them until I cried out; and then his member was in my open mouth, cutting off the sound and filling it up. I choked, my eyes watering. My hands scrabbled at his knees and he pulled my head back, giving me a chance to breathe. "Suck my cock." My body ripened at the sound of his coarse language, and I took a deep breath before he shoved my face forward again, filling up my mouth.

It was all I could do to keep breathing and not choke on the saliva that pooled and spilled out the corners of my mouth, to keep my tongue covering my teeth – I knew enough to guess that he didn't want to be bitten – and let him direct me, pleasuring himself with my lips and tongue. He tasted salty, and bitter – a little like the water around here, a little like the oil I'd scented on him earlier. I closed my eyes and concentrated on breathing, on not biting down, even when I was afraid I was going to vomit. Impatient, he stood up, and began thrusting with his hips while he held my head still. My insides felt hot and liquid. I gagged and wiggled, my hands tangled in his pants to keep myself from falling.

His voice was a low murmur. "Anyone can see you." My eyes flew open, and I realized the door was still open. Humiliation flooded my body and I moaned, but he smiled. "I like the sounds you make. Be a good slave and moan for me." I whimpered against his thrusting cock, my body hot and ripe. "Don't you want to show the governor what a good little slave you are, sucking your owner's cock?" I couldn't help it. I moaned again, mortified and wet. His thrusts sped up. "And if you please me, I might see my way clear to pleasing you back. You like my fingers in your cunt, don't you, little slave?" I groaned at the memory flooding my senses, the arousal that spiked at his words. "But if you don't please me, I'll just flip you over my knee and spank you again." Fear seemed to heat my insides even more, and my aching bottom throbbed at the reminder. I groaned, trying to plead with him, but I couldn't form words with his cock filling my mouth and brushing the back of my throat with every thrust. His next words were tight and breathy. "If you want to please me, be a good little slave, and swallow it all." My eyes flew open and I stared into his, afraid I wouldn't be able to do it, not with drool dripping off my chin. He groaned and rammed in until my lips pressed against his curly hair and he thickened, pulsing with his orgasm. I struggled, my throat hurting, but his hand was iron, holding me down on his cock until he finished and I gagged, choking, swallowing desperately. When he released me, I coughed, trying to swallow all the fluid in my mouth, but some spilled. I wiped my chin hurriedly, hoping he hadn't seen it. But he did. A finger tipped my chin up and I flushed, caught.

"Clean your fingers off."

I hesitated, then reached for my dress.

"No. Lick them off. Wipe your face with your fingers and lick them." I shook, more embarrassed than I'd ever been, and unbelievably aroused. I obeyed, tasting his hot bitter cum, my own saliva. I wiped my streaming eyes and nose, and this time he handed me a handkerchief. Grateful, I finished cleaning my face.

I watched him with wide eyes. "Are... are you pleased?"

He grinned at me. "I am pleased."

I relaxed, slumping down in my relief.

"But not so pleased you are going to escape a spanking." The bolt of heat his words sent through my insides seemed contrary to the fear that bloomed in my belly, but he didn't seem to care about either. He lifted me, tucking me between his knees and laying me over his left knee, my upper body draped on his bed. It was so soft I might have sighed in pleasure if I hadn't been so worried about the hand that was flipping the fabric off my bottom. He squeezed my buttocks and I cried out, the throb intensifying.

"Good girl, Nanette. I'm not angry with you. So this is just a little spanking."

I whimpered, reassured. His hand lifted, and spanked down hard. I squealed, wriggling like a fish on a hook. He pressed down on my back, pinning me to his bed, and spanked me again. Again, again, until I had a dozen new handprints on my already red bottom and the throbbing felt louder than my heartbeat. He released me, and I lay still, afraid to move, my whole body painted in shades of heat. He lifted my right leg and shifted me, so that my thighs straddled his left thigh, leaving my vulva open to his perusal. I squirmed, the throb spreading to my swollen lips. He slid a finger along my slit, and I could feel the wetness coating it.

"Such a good slave," he murmured, and it almost undid me. I tried to wiggle away from him, but he held my hips down with his left hand, and slid more fingers along my slit, spreading my thick lips and coating them with the copious moisture my body produced. I stuffed some of the blanket from the bed in my mouth to stifle the cries his teasing fingers inspired. He found the little nub where my pleasure centered and circled it, again and again and again, refusing to touch it. I panted, shifting my hips, desperate for greater intensity. His finger left me and I moaned, and then he flicked my clitoris, the sensation sharp and shocking. I shrieked, a blaze of arousal threatening to consume me. He resumed circling it. I moaned, dejected and helpless. I could feel the liquid sliding from my vagina to my clitoris, soaking into my own curls.

"Such an eager little clit." His voice was mocking, and I whimpered. "Such a wet cunt." I flushed red, unable to focus on anything other than need. "Tell me."

"Sir?"

"Tell me your clit is eager."

"My – my clit is – is eager."

"Eager for what?"

"Eager for – for – for – your finger."

He flicked it again and I cringed, panting. "Like that?"

"N-n-no – no! Not – not – that."

"Oh?" He flicked it again, and I gasped, my hips gyrating on his thigh.

"You clit is so swollen. I think it likes it."

"No-no-no-"

He flicked it again.

"OH! Oh, oh, oh!" I could feel the lubrication pouring out of my cunt. My thighs tightened on his, desperately trying to tip my hips down so I could press the swollen nub against something solid, something that would ease the need.

"No, little slave. You get what pleasure I give you. No relief without me. You understand?"

I moaned, the wave of need tumbling me under. He pressed his broad thumb against my clit then, the pressure on my button triggering wild flailing of my limbs. He held my hips down, blocking my hands with his shoulder, and ground his thumb into my oversensitive nub of flesh. I wailed, and then he started rubbing in a circle. I erupted, all heat and molten liquid and high volume. I groaned with the exquisite release – it was like nothing I'd ever experienced in my life.

When it was over, I lay limp on his bed, still draped over his knee. I wasn't sure I could move if I wanted to, but I didn't want to.

My cunt twitched with emptiness, but I wasn't sure I cared. His hand stroked my bottom, smoothing the handprints of my second spanking.

"Good girl." His pride wrapped itself around my heart and I wondered again if it would be worth belonging to him, if he could make me feel this way.

CHAPTER
FOUR

WHEN I HAD RECOVERED ENOUGH to move, Jeffery lifted me to standing, and kissed my forehead. "You belong to me, Nanette. Now you will have to work for the House, to earn your keep, as do I. I have work to do today. Lauren will be in charge of you while I am not available. I expect to hear a good report when I come back this evening. If I do, I will bring you to my bed tonight. If I do not, I will spank you and you will sleep in the kitchen. Do you understand?"

I nodded, still drained from my recent pleasure, but my bottom throbbed. "Yes, sir." I definitely wanted more time in his bed, and didn't want to be spanked any more.

"Roy, of course, has the authority to do anything he wants with you, whether it is work anywhere in our territory, or work in his bed." I cocked my head at him, unsure I liked this train of conversation. He ignored me. "Lauren has authority to order you to do any work that needs to be done, and she has permission to punish you as she sees fit if you do not obey. You understand?"

"Yes, sir."

He kissed me on the forehead again. "Go to the kitchen now."

I hesitated, then nodded. "Yes, sir." I felt his eyes on my body as I left the room.

Passing through the open door, I remembered my squeals and

groans, how anyone could have heard them. Fear seized my heart as I wondered what Suzanna had heard, what she was thinking. The dining room was empty when I entered, and Lauren was the only one in the kitchen. I looked around, the fear making me bold. "Where is Suzanna?"

Lauren looked up from chopping the onions. "I sent her to rearrange the pantry building with Jacqueline." She brushed my hair away from my face in an unexpectedly tender gesture, and it reminded me of my mother. My heart constricted. "I thought you might prefer she not hear that."

My face flushed hot again, and I stared at the floor, humiliated, but grateful. "Thank you."

"You weren't a virgin, were you?"

I bit my lip, still embarrassed. "No, ma'am."

She nodded, satisfied. "Good. I didn't think he'd be that rough if you were, but I wanted to check."

For some reason, I felt compelled to defend the man who'd given me pleasure beyond anything I'd ever known before. "He isn't that rough. At least... not... all the time. Just when he... spanks me. Or..." I remembered choking on his cock. "...when he... he... puts it in my mouth."

She snorted. "When he face fucks you."

I wasn't sure I could survive this conversation without dying of mortification. "Y...yes."

She snorted again. "I'm glad you find it pleasurable."

For a moment I was stymied. Did I find it pleasurable? I remembered the gasping, the tears streaming down my face, the drool dripping off my chin, the gagging. If it wasn't pleasurable, why was my body acting like it was ready for another round with his thumb? I shivered, wrapping my arms around myself. Her voice broke into my thoughts.

"Well, don't just stand there. Make yourself useful."

I hurried to the chopping block, and she handed me a basket full of potatoes. "Scrub. Chop. Trim as sparingly as you can. Pile them into this pot when you're finished."

"Yes, ma'am."

I was nearly finished filling the large pot, my hands aching from the unaccustomed labor when Suzanna came in. She gave me a quick hug as she passed, carrying a basket full of some sort of squash in a variety of colors. "I hope this is the right amount. Jacqueline wasn't sure how many of the men would be eating dinner here today."

"We'll make food for the larger number of whoever is likely to be. If they don't get back in time for dinner, we'll save it for them and they can eat it for supper."

"Okay."

I finished the potatoes and Lauren set it on the stove, filling it with water to cover. I looked at the jug of water she set down. "Is that straight from the river?"

She snorted. "Of course not. It's filtered and boiled first. That's why it's in the jugs." I nodded, remembering the way my mother had explained that you needed to do that with some rivers. We were lucky – where we grew up the river was pure and clear, so she would just fill buckets from the little waterfall north of our place and lug them back home. I remembered how proud I was the first day I was big enough to help her. "We'll need to do a batch today, just like every day. You'll help."

I nodded. "Yes, ma'am."

The morning went by quickly. I was as careful as I could be to hide my winces when my sore bottom was bumped, and Suzanna seemed to settle in faster than I thought she would. But then, helping out in Lauren's kitchen was a lot more like home than hiking through endless forests had been. Jacqueline helped, listless and lifeless, hurrying only when Lauren spoke sharply to her. I worried about her, if she was being abused, to cause such abject misery.

My arms were aching by the time dinner was ready. Hefting jug after jug of water, chopping vegetables and fruits, stirring huge pots and ladling hot preserves into ceramic jars was far more labor than I was accustomed to at home. Still, I was grateful for the lull, the opportunity to settle in and make myself useful. Suzanna never complained, and obeyed Lauren flawlessly, which surprised me at least a little.

It wasn't until we were sitting next to each other, quietly eating dinner when I found out why.

Lauren had spoken first. "You've done very well this morning, Suzanna." She smiled, and my heart swelled with her dimples.

I chimed in. "I'm proud of you, little sister." She smiled at me too. "I think even Mom would be surprised at how hard you've worked today." Her smile faltered, and I regretted reminding her of the uncertain loss.

Lauren crossed her arms over her chest, leaning back and contemplating my sister. "We reached an understanding this morning, Suzanna and I, didn't we, girl?"

She blushed now, and looked away. I frowned, not liking the tone Lauren was using.

I leaned forward, my voice rising to demand. "What do you mean, an understanding?" Lauren raised an eyebrow at me and I sat back, chastened.

"Suzanna learned that children are not exempt from corporal punishment in this house."

"What?" I stood up, outraged.

Lauren simply eyed me. Jacqueline looked up, and then her blank gaze slid off, uncaring.

"Don't act so indignant. She told me you were both spanked at home. It's not a big deal." My face flamed, and my buttocks throbbed. It was a big deal, if my own spankings were any indication – and I deflated abruptly. I realized what Lauren was trying to tell me. Suzanna was a child. She hadn't been subjected to anywhere near the harshness I had been. In fact – I eyed her – she seemed to be sitting quite comfortably. I released the breath I'd been about to yell with. There was structure, and hierarchy, and discipline in this house, so she'd been informed of her place within it. I took another breath.

"You're okay?" I couldn't help but touch her shoulder in concern, but she shrugged me off, teenage mortification all over her face.

"Yeah, of course. No big deal." She tossed her head and I half smiled, reassured. Her ego might have been bruised, but that was about it.

Roy was absent from dinner, as were Jeffery and Devon. Curious, I asked Lauren about the last man's name.

She pointed to the man next to Tobin. "That's Gerard, Tobin's half brother."

After dinner, the absent men's dinners packed up and put away for them, Lauren handed Jacqueline and me pails of soapy water and a variety of rags. "You, upstairs." Jacqueline turned to obey, and Lauren pointed to me. "You, downstairs. Start at the far end of the hall. Don't do the dungeon, start with the bathing room first. When you've done that, come back here for instructions on the other rooms. There are different rules for each of them."

I stood for a moment, unsure if there were further directions, but she snapped a towel at me. "Shoo! Get moving."

I jumped, and hurried towards the hall, careful not to spill the bucket.

I found the bathing room. It was lined with ceramic – a pattern of small tiles in different colors on the walls and floor. A large window looked out on the land surrounding the building. I leaned out, letting the breeze ruffle my hair and tease my skin. I looked down. The ground nearby was pebbly, and in the distance I could see the river forking around the ground. If I squinted, I thought perhaps the stand of rocks hid a building of some sort. Movement caught my eye, and I saw a man with a weapon in his hands, walking slowly along, as if he were patrolling. Maybe he was? Maybe the building was on an island in the river, and they were guarding it? I hadn't had any chance to look around when we'd first arrived. I tried to remember the ancient map Daddy had in his study, if there was a broad river with islands on the way to Caladonia. Once again I lamented the misfortune of our map – and wondered what had happened to our packs.

Sighing, I turned my attention back to the room. There were two chamber pots, a large barrel of what appeared to be clean water, and a pipe that looked like it led to the river outside. That, I surmised, was for the piss. There was a toilet seat in the corner, a tall basket filled with plant material and wood shavings directly beside it, and two closed pots beside that. Nature called, and I decided to relieve myself before cleaning. Lifting the toilet I saw it was very like the one I'd grown up with, down to the small step on the front that put my knees higher than my hips. The dress was easy enough to pull around my body, and after I was finished, I wiped with a clean cloth from the stack beside the seat, and reached for the pots. The larger pot was full, presumably matching the one currently in the toilet I was seated on, and the smaller one was what I was looking for – a soaking bin for used cloths. I tossed in the cloth and closed it again, then stood up. There was a small basin with soapy water in it, so I washed, then poured it down the pipe. Drying my hands on a towel hung on a peg, I refilled the basin for the next person with a scoop from the barrel, and looked around for the soap. After a bit I realized there were shelves behind me, and there was a jar of tiny round soap beads. I dropped one in the basin, then took a scoop of the plant bits and wood shavings, sprinkling them generously on the contents of the toilet pot before closing the lid.

I turned back to my cleaning pail. I wondered if Lauren intended for me to clean the chamber pots also, and decided that I ought to show I could be proactive. I decided to leave them for last, however, and start with the great wooden tubs in the corner. They were tipped up on their sides, and didn't seem to need any washing, but I didn't want anyone to say I wasn't earning my keep. So I took out the largest rag and wiped them down with the soapy water from my pail, rinsing them out with clean water from the barrel, as little as I could manage. After spending most of the morning on sterilizing water for use I had no inclination to waste a drop more than necessary down the pipe. Leaving them in the middle of the bathing room, I washed down the shelves, shifting the contents back and forth, then washed around the basin and the table it was set on.

Returning to the corner the tubs lived in, I washed the walls, standing up on my tiptoes to reach as high as I could, and stooping to reach all the way down to the edge of the floor, continuing around the room.

One wall was set with a large mirror, and I paused, looking at my reflection. My hair was jagged – early on in our run, I'd realized I didn't want to deal with my long hair, so I'd gathered it up in one hand and hacked it off with the knife in my other. It had grown out a little since then, but it was still short. The blonde was variegated, of inconsistent shades, sun streaked. My eyes were red-rimmed and dark shadowed – no wonder Suzanna was worried about me. My lips were still swollen from Jeffery's pleasure, and I touched them gently, smoothing my fingertips over the dark pink flesh. I tried on a smile. It didn't help much, but maybe a little.

I took out another rag and washed down the toilet seat and the outsides of the pots and basket. I started to wash the floor, and the tails of my dress got in the way. Not wanting it to be wet or dirty, I found myself tying the length around my legs to keep it up as I worked. I washed the floor from one corner almost to the door, returning the tubs to their corner and leaving myself room to get to the pipe. My water was looking decidedly grayer by this point, so I washed the chamber pots, adding an additional tiny soap into each one before pouring in some water from my bucket. Finishing the chamber pots, I emptied them down the pipe and wiped down the outsides, setting them back where they were. Then I took a final rag and washed the floor as I backed out on my hands and knees. Upon reaching the door, I realized I'd forgotten to put the cleaning rags into the soaking pot, so I took a couple cautious steps forward, hoping my knees were clean enough not to mar the freshly washed floor, and tossed them in. Finally, I sat back on my heels and surveyed the bathroom. It was satisfactory to my eyes, and I hoped Lauren would agree. For a moment, I remembered my mother's voice, instructing Suzanna and me on washing our bathroom, and then it morphed into her voice, the urgency in it as she told me not to look back, not to wait for her, not to stop. To go and keep going, to take care of Suzanna. I looked at my hands, wrinkly from the water. I'm trying, Mom. I'm trying. This isn't quite the way you wanted me to take care of her, but it's the best I can do right now.

It wasn't until Lauren came to find me that I realized tears were tracking down my face, dampening the top of my dress.

She squatted down beside me, taking my chin and turning my face towards hers. "Everyone has a history. Everyone has pain. Like it or not, for better or worse, your future is tied to this House now."

I couldn't meet her eyes. I didn't feel like it should be – our future had been tied to this house by force, by happenstance, not by choice. Or, if there was a choice, it was the choice to choose the known fear over the unknown one. She shook me a little.

"Look at me, girl."

I raised my eyes, rebelliousness in my mouth.

She half-smiled. "For what it's worth, this is a good one, a better one than the majority of the ones you could have stumbled on. You could have been killed, or taken as a slave by a pimp, tied down and raped hourly in one of the bigger towns." I blanched, shivering despite the warmth of the air. "Here, you are valued. You are worth more than a momentary pleasure. Don't forget it."

The set of my mouth softened, and my shoulders slumped. She was right. I straightened up again. I would do better. I would please them, show them they were right to keep me. I swallowed. "Thank you, ma'am."

She patted my cheek. "That a girl. Up you go."

She helped me up and I remembered my skirts tied awkwardly around my legs. "Leave it."

I obeyed, hefting the bucket and taking it back to the kitchen where she poured it out the pipe there. She filled it again with water and soap, and then pointed out the broom and dusting rags. "You're going to start with Jeffery's room. That way if you mess up, you won't get in trouble with two men, just Jeffery. Now, wash the shutters first. Then dust and polish all the furniture. Don't take anything, don't break anything, and if you see something that seems to need attention, tell me. Replace the cloths pot with a clean one."

She handed me a small ceramic pot with a lid. "And strip the linens off the bed. Fluff the mattress, then put clean linens on the bed. You'll find them in the hallway closet. Finally, sweep the room, and wash the floor. Any questions?"

I shook my head. "No, ma'am."

"Shoo."

I turned quickly, trying to balance everything without dropping it, and returned to the hall. There, I hesitated. Was his room the third down or the fourth? I cautiously opened the fourth, and was relieved to see my guess was correct. Remembering his admonition to earn a good report, I set to work.

The bed dominated the room. It was huge, with a large latticed headboard and footboard. The mattress was thick, and I wondered if they'd made it themselves, and if so, how long it had taken to collect the feathers. Or if they bought it. The shutters were mostly closed, and the room smelled of sex and sweat that made me blush. I washed the shutters quickly, then pushed them open, letting in a gust of fresh air. It smelled of the river, and I smiled for a moment, reminded of home and safety. The feeling faded as the breeze died, but I pressed on, determined.

There were hooks on the wall – a series of big ones that held another pair of overalls and another shirt, and a series of massive ones that held nothing. I touched one, a prickling feeling in my spine. I had to reach up to touch them, and they were so solid... I turned away, focusing on the business at hand. Wiping them down, I continued on to the wardrobe. It was wood, and again, I wondered at the wealth this House seemed to command. Either the members were very talented at making things, or they had things of high value to trade. There was a smaller wooden chest beside the wardrobe, and I polished it as well. The cloths pot I found near the head of the bed, the lid askew, the handkerchief I'd wiped my face with peeking out. I blushed again, remembering the feel of his hand in my hair, his cock in my mouth and down my throat. I brushed my fingertips over my lips, and I found myself ripening, desiring

47

his attention as my mind drifted back over the explosive pleasure his fingers could trigger.

Shaking myself, I forced myself back to work. Stripping the bed was difficult alone, but I managed eventually, leaving the linens in a heap on the floor. Making it back up again was worse – I'd always hated doing it, trying to remember how to tuck the corners so it wouldn't come undone. Given how it was tucked to start with, I couldn't imagine that tossing a blanket on it and calling it good would work. So I struggled, tugging and straightening and tucking, then redoing it, until I had it as even as I could manage. I wiped my sweaty forehead with the back of my hand and surveyed my work. It wasn't completely even – I jammed a bit of one corner under the mattress again and hoped it wouldn't show – but it wasn't horrible. I hoped. Kicking the linens into the hallway, rolling up the carpet to take outside and beat, I began to sweep. There was sand, and bits of dirt and vegetation. I made a tidy pile and realized I'd forgotten the dustpan. So I returned to the kitchen and grabbed it.

There was a new woman in the kitchen. I didn't wait to be introduced, merely bobbed a half acknowledgment - "Ma'am" - and continued back to Jeffery's room. Once I'd gotten the detritus swept up, I realized I had no idea where it was supposed to go. Mom used to just toss it out the door – there wasn't a door here, but there was a window. Unsure if I was doing the right thing or not, I crossed the room quickly and dumped the pan out the window. Setting both broom and pan in the hallway, I started washing the floor under the window, steadily working my way back to the door.

I heard his footsteps before I heard his voice. I'd just backed into the hallway on my knees, my arms stretched in front of myself, wet with cleaning water, the skirt still tied around my thighs.

"Nanette."

I whirled around, my heart thumping.

"Yes, sir?"

Jeffery dropped to a knee behind me, his fingers unerringly finding the crease in my buttocks, sliding down to my vulva, pressing my dress in until it dampened with anticipation. His fingers pressed against my bottom hole and I flinched. He pressed harder.

"Mine."

My voice was a whisper, humiliation and fear warring with recognition of the pleasure he gave me. "Yes, sir."

"I hope you're being a good girl, Nanette."

I nodded frantically. "Yes, sir! I am!"

"Good. Because I want you in my bed tonight. If you aren't there, I will be very disappointed."

"Yes, sir!"

"You don't want to disappoint me, do you, Nanette?"

"No! No sir!"

His teasing fingers left me and returned with a resounding slap. I flinched and whimpered.

"I don't have time to play now." His voice was regretful. "But I will play with you later. If you're a good girl."

"Yes, sir!"

He stood and walked into the room, removing something from his trunk and returning. I stared in dismay at the footprints he left on the just washed floor.

He saw my expression and leaned over, grabbing a handful of my hair and tipping my head so he could whisper in my ear. "Be a good little slave and wash it again." I couldn't say why his words and his hot breath in my ear excited me, but they did. He was gone before I had the presence of mind to do more than kneel there, blinking against the blinding arousal.

And so I returned to the kitchen and asked for a fresh bucket of wash water for Jeffery's room. Lauren raised an eyebrow. I answered, my voice low. "He told me to wash it again." Even saying the words thickened my nether lips – obeying the man who claimed me seemed a greater thing than obeying the woman who ruled the kitchen. I returned to the room and started under the window again, lingering on each footprint, careful to leave no trace of dirt on the floor.

When it was finished, Lauren showed me where to leave the

dirty linens and gave the rug to a man outside to beat clean. She gave me directions for the other men's rooms, but I flew through them, paying very little attention. My mind was preoccupied by Jeffery's threat, by his promise. I found that even the slightest movement of fabric on my nipples drove them into hard points, and the fabric tied up around my thighs had shifted, grazing my swollen lips with a brazenness I didn't know clothing could possess.

CHAPTER
FIVE

SUPPER WAS CROWDED. The table was filled with men, and this time I saw that there were other women. Some wore clothing similar to mine, and some were dressed more like Suzanna or Lauren. I had untied my skirts, smoothing the crumpled cloth as much as possible – not much – and jumped at every chance to take something to the table. There were new women in the kitchen, too, all of them dressed like myself.

Roy stood up at the head of the table and the place fell quiet. "Suzanna! Come here."

My sister went, blushing at becoming the center of attention.

"This girl is my latest ward. She will stay in Marcus's family, with his daughters, to be cared for as his own."

A few claps, a few handshakes, and the man who must be Marcus, broad with dark hair, nodded, solemn and delighted. The woman next to him seemed to be his wife; she smiled cheerfully at Suzanna. My heart constricted. Where did they live? Where did they come from? How would I see her? I'd lived with her, day in, day out, for the last fourteen years. How could I stand to be separated from her now? At least they didn't seem cruel, I reminded myself. At least she would have other girls around her. Still, my hands balled into fists and I bit my lip to keep from crying. She seemed less shocked than I was, and I remembered the woman in the kitchen. Had this been discussed while I was washing Jeffery's room and longing for his bed? Was I a terrible elder sister, for not paying better attention?

Too soon, she was seated between them, nervous but smiling.

Roy quieted them again. "Nanette!"

I went to him, stumbling. He dragged the padlock on my neck chain around so everyone could see it.

"This woman is my slave. I have given her service to Jeffery."

Louder cheers, a few hoots and hollers. Jeffery rose, then stood behind me, his arms wrapping around my waist. Despite his looming menace, I felt a measure of safety there. I didn't know the men in the dining room. I barely knew Jeffery. But I trusted my place with him. I understood what I had to do to stay in his favor, and when I did, he gave me pleasure, gave me certainty. His hand under my chin lifted it, and I felt my nervousness replaced with a measure of pride. Obviously he was known to these men, and they seemed pleased that he had been rewarded with me. Even the women smiled. Except Stephanie. But I was rather glad she didn't – her smiles seemed to indicate the opposite of most peoples'.

Roy sat down. Jeffery did also, a few seats away, and pushed me down onto a cushion at his feet. I obeyed, my heart beating wildly at the thought of all the people seeing me, eating under the table like an animal. He caressed my hair, and when the plates were brought out, he leaned over to set one on the floor for me. I stared at it, my stomach tight with hunger and queasy with humiliation. What did he expect me to do? Eat it with my mouth like a dog? My lips trembled and I looked up, eyes wide and pleading. He picked up the spoon from beside his plate and passed it down to me with a wink. I gasped, overcome with relief.

Leaning forward onto one elbow, I ate with the spoon, trying to hide it, trying not to watch the other women under the table who ate with their mouths in the plates. Stephanie was one of them, and she shot me a venomous look when she caught sight of the spoon. I looked away, and noticed that only the women who had chains with padlocks on their necks were under the table. The other half of the women had medallions, and had remained seated. A brief stab of envy caught me in the stomach and I stopped eating for a moment. Closing my eyes, I inhaled the spicy scent of the fish stew, the vegetables, and wondered if it would taste better on top of the table or not.

Jeffery's hand caressed my shoulders then, and I looked up. He wasn't looking at me, just eating, absently petting me with his free hand. I stayed still for a long minute, watching him talk and laugh with the others at the table. Was this all my life was going to be? A pet? A slave who did menial chores and pleased his cock? He glanced down, feeling my eyes on him, and his fingers caught my ear, rubbing it until I mewed with pleasure. Was that such a horrible fate, if it was?

Supper finally ended. I watched the other women lounge under the table, having their own whispered conversations with each other while the ones seated at the table conversed. Alone, I got bored, and finally lapsed into memories of our hike, trying to recreate the path we'd traveled, trying to figure out where we'd gone wrong on the way to Caladonia.

Abruptly, Jeffery stood up, startling me. I came to attention, knocking my head on the underside of the table and yelping. He reached down, rubbing my head. His voice in my ear again. "Poor little slave. That's not a good pain, is it? I can give you a better one." My body reacted positively, and I whimpered, just a little. He snapped his fingers, and I followed him, crawling, uncertain if I should stand. No one said anything about it, so I continued to crawl as the conversations swirled nonchalantly around me. I risked a glance at Suzanna. She was talking to the woman who would be taking care of her, and didn't seem to have noticed me. Good. I continued following Jeffery to his room.

He was taking off his clothes when I got there, hanging them on the hooks. This time, he closed the door. I knelt, watching him. He was muscular, and his thick cock was already hard, standing at attention. I licked my lips, remembering his harsh attentions. He turned to me. "Strip."

I obeyed, unclipping the chain around my waist and carefully folding up the cloth strips, leaving the knots as they were. He pointed to the bed. "Here."

I climbed up, breathless with anticipation. Would he fuck me now? I realized I'd wanted it since the first time I came around his fingers.

He shoved me face first into the mattress, the sheets I'd put on the bed just earlier. My bottom high in the air, I whimpered, uncertain. Would he spank me? And I found the thought – while frightening – was not abhorrent. His fingers traced my crease and I tensed, my bottom hole tightening. He chuckled, and pressed a dry finger against it.

"You belong to me. Every part of you, even your ass." I whimpered. He slid his fingers lower, dipping them into my cunt until I relaxed, pressing back against his hand. "Your cunt is mine. Your lips are mine. Your clit is mine." His free hand slid up my flank to where my heavy breasts fell to the bed and reached under them, pinching one nipple, then the other. "Your nipples are mine." I moaned, my hips rocking with the pleasure he drew out of my body. "When you clean. When you cook. When you eat. When you poop. You are mine." I wiggled, embarrassment flooding my chest. "When did you poop last?" I bit my lip, mortified. His hand left my cunt and slapped down hard on my sore bottom. I jerked away, whimpering. "You answer any question I ask, immediately." I cried out, wordlessly protesting his demand. He slapped me again, but I mewed, not answering. Impatient, he shoved me forward on the bed, then spanked my thighs until I started to cry. His voice in my ear again. "I don't care how embarrassed you are. You answer. Or you will be spanked until you do. Do you understand?"

I nodded. "Yes, sir." Sniffling, I looked up at him, hoping the plea in my wide eyes would soften his heart. Not this time. He pulled my thighs apart and spanked the tender inner sides until I begged him to stop. "Please, sir!"

He stopped. "When did you poop last?"

I bit my lip, took a deep breath. "Shortly after dinner, sir."

He stroked my burning thighs, smoothing the sting. "Good girl."

I wiggled at his praise, wondering what had possessed him to ask such a question. He lifted me back onto my knees again, and suddenly my stomach dropped. Surely he didn't intend – couldn't possibly intend – wouldn't, really, would he?

He slammed his fingers into my cunt again and I sagged, relief flooding through me. I moaned, reveling in the pleasure his hand could bring. In so short a time I'd been reduced to this – wanting his touch like nothing else. I could feel my juices coating his hand, wet and dripping. He withdrew, and I gasped, needy.

His fingers pressed against my bottom hole and I cried out, all my unanswered questions suddenly answered at once. Yes, yes, he would.

A finger pressed hard and I panted, tight with distaste and fear. His voice was in my ear. "Relax. Be a good little slave and open up."

It heated my insides, and before I knew it, I found myself obeying, relaxing that tight ring of muscle and trying to open up for his finger. It slipped in, my own lubrication easing the way. I gasped, moaning softly at the strange invasion. It felt intimate, violating my most private body part. His finger moved then, sliding in and out, stroking the sensitive walls. I cried out. It hurt, but it felt good at the same time. So very very wrong – and yet, it was sending out ripples of pleasure.

Is there anything more humiliating than a finger in your bottom? I found out that yes, there was.

"Good little slave. Good girl, Nanette. I'm going to take my finger out now, and I'm going to put my cock inside you. I want you to open up and bear down." His cock nudged my tight hole, smearing its own lubrication on my flesh, and I flushed red. He slid fingers from his other hand into my cunt, dipping them in and using the juice to stroke himself, painting himself with my lubrication. I squeezed my eyes shut, and he pressed harder, demanding entrance. "Open up like a good little slave. You know you want to feel my hard cock inside you." The greatest humiliation was knowing that it was true. I really did want to know what it felt like, his hard length buried inside me.

"Open up. Relax." I took a deep breath, reminded myself that I belonged to him, and opened my bottom hole as wide as I could. "Good girl."

The smooth head of his cock pressed in, and I suddenly felt so full I couldn't bear it. I cried out, gasping and twisting away from him.

"No. Stop. You'll hurt yourself if you do that. Just relax."

I listened, whimpering my pain and fear, but I obeyed. He pressed deeper, and I tried to relax as much as I could. With a sudden slide, he was seated fully in my ass. I moaned, clenching around him. He petted my hip, his fingers damp with the soapy cloth he'd used to wash them. "Good girl. You're such a good girl."

I whimpered, and he slid out a little ways. I gasped. The feeling reminded me too much of relieving myself and I gagged in disgust. Then he slid in again, and the sensation strummed my nerves. Thrusting in and out, his thickness seemed to find a point of pleasure I didn't know was there and rubbed against it. I moaned, dazed by the unaccustomed sensation, the strange intensity of the pleasure. He caught my hips, and began to pound into me, hard, fucking my ass like he had my face.

Unlike my face, there was no ambiguity in this pleasure. It radiated, twisting around my core and turning me to a flopping rag doll of need, begging incoherently for more until he touched off something deep inside me, sending me into a fountain of loud pleasure. When I clenched down, my body trying to wring every last drop of sensation from him, he erupted inside me. I could feel the heat of his cum as it shot in deep. I groaned, collapsing bonelessly on the bed.

He softened and we lay together, my ass stretched and full, his cock gradually shrinking back to its sleeping size. When it was smaller, he slid out of me and I moaned, shocked at how empty it made me feel. My cunt ached, and he reached around me for the soapy cloths he'd prepared. Washing his cock off, he tossed the cloth in the pot beside the bed, then wrapped his arms around me. I dozed, worn out from work and pleasure.

Some time later, the door opened softly and I awoke with a start. Jeffery was snoring quietly beside me. I gathered the sheet up to my chest.

"May I come in?"

I recognized Suzanna's voice. "Of course!"

She tiptoed in, and it was then that I saw Marcus's wife standing outside the door. Suzanna sat on the edge of the bed, and I bit my lip, ashamed for her to see me here, obviously disheveled from the man's bed. The moon lit up the room with a pale light, and I hoped she didn't see much.

"I'm supposed to go with Marcus and Julia tonight. They live on the same island we're on, just the other side of it."

I nodded, relieved to hear she wasn't going as far as I thought. "Good. I hope you have a good time with their daughters."

"I hope so." We sat together for a long minute. "They aren't going to be my parents, not really. Just until Daddy and Mom get here."

I bit down hard enough on my lip to draw blood, sucking it before she noticed. "They can never replace Daddy and Mom, no. But Suzanna, I don't know if Daddy and Mom will ever find us."

She shook her head, stubborn. "They'll find us."

I swallowed hard. "Okay. You go with them. Be good. I'll visit you as often as I can."

She touched her forehead to mine. "Okay."

"I love you."

"I love you, too."

She rose and Julia tucked her under an arm. "Don't worry, Nanette. We'll take good care of her." I nodded, a lump in my throat. They left, closing the door behind them.

After a long minute, I lay back down beside the man who'd claimed me.

CHAPTER
SIX

DAWN FOUND me wrapped inside a pair of brawny arms. At first I jerked away, still foggy with sleep, but his voice, gravelly and soft, brought me back to the present. "Go back to sleep, little slave."

I settled against him, my heart beating fast against my ribs. For a long moment I could not relax, worried about Suzanna, worried about Daddy, worried about Mom. His lips brushed the back of my head, and I realized he had never kissed me. I twisted around until I could face him, craning my neck.

I meant to ask what he expected of me, how I could best please him, but what came out instead was, "Why did you want to keep me?"

He opened his eyes. "Because you're beautiful."

For a moment I was crestfallen. It was only the sex, then.

"Because you fought like a cougar to defend your sister."

I looked back up at him. "What if I hadn't?"

He shrugged. "I might have asked for a day to use you. But I wouldn't have asked to keep you."

"Why not?"

"This is a hard world. Women are vulnerable. But women who succumb too easily are even more vulnerable. I wouldn't want to share my room with a woman who would roll over at the slightest threat."

"But I did. Submit easily. I mean I do."

He stroked my hair. "Yes. And that's what I want. You fought, when there was a chance of freedom. But once you realized there wasn't, you obeyed. Practicality, adaptability – these will help you survive in this world."

"What if I don't want to survive here?"

He shrugged. "You're safer here than anywhere else. Your sister is safer here than anywhere else."

I started to say home was even safer, but then I remembered my parents' words, and bit back the thought. Maybe he was right.

"I own you now, and I protect what is mine."

I dropped my head, considering his words. I remembered Daddy's instructions. *Love someone who can protect you.* Could I love this man?

His fingers stopped my thoughts in their tracks as he eased them between my thighs, spreading my legs and caressing my lips, pinching them together and rubbing. My sensitive nub woke up and swelled, his fingers tight as they rolled back and forth, back and forth over the bump between them. I squirmed. He nuzzled my face, his breath hot in my ear. "How wet is my little slave? Would you like my fingers inside you?"

I arched off the bed, my hips pressing towards his hand. "Yes. Please. Yes, sir."

He released my hot flesh and I whimpered. Sliding a single finger between my thick lips, he grinned. "You're wet, little slave. But I don't think you're wet enough yet."

I arched towards him again, trying to get more pressure from his fingers.

"No, Nanette. Lie still."

I obeyed, my breath coming quickly as he shifted, looming over me. His head dipped to my heavy breasts and then his mouth closed over a nipple. I shrieked, arching off the bed towards the shocking sensation.

"Oh, oh, oh!"

He released it and growled at me. "I told you to lie still."

His voice sent shivers through my body, and it was all I could do to lay flat. His mouth captured the other nipple, and his tongue teased it, flicking the hard flesh until I couldn't think. He released it, then turned back to the first one, biting and licking my breast. My hands fisted in the sheets, desperate to obey. When he was satisfied that I was nearly out of my mind with exquisite sensation, he started on the other. I wailed, panting with need. Having bound my breasts for years, they had been protected from the harshness of clothing, and he ruthlessly exploited that tenderness.

Jeffrey shifted his elbows closer to my body and grabbed handfuls of ample flesh, squeezing and caressing. His voice was low. "How wet is my little slave now?"

I moaned, too lost in the feel of his calloused hands rasping over my soft skin to answer. He pinched hard on my nipples, and order forgotten, I arched off the bed, keening. His voice rasped against my ear again. "Did I tell you to move? Or did I tell you to lie still?"

I panted. "So – so-sorry. Still. I'll – lie still."

He grinned then, the cruel predatory grin he'd first frightened me with on the boat. "Of course you will. After I punish you for disobeying me."

I cried out as his fingers tightened, pain shooting through my breasts. "Please! I'll be – be good."

He sat up, releasing me, and I heaved a sigh. But my relief was short-lived. Grasping the areola between his thick fingers, he lifted my left breast until I squealed, struggling to keep my body flat on the bed. His other hand slapped the underside, sending the flesh to jiggling, a burning handprint throbbing on my skin. I wailed. He slapped it again, and again. Tears filled my eyes. He released my breast and it flopped back down. Pinching the areola of my right breast, he pulled it away from my body, exposing the tender underside. I wailed, knowing what was going to happen, desperate to be still and obey anyway. The slaps stung and my flesh bounced, a riot of sensations concentrated in my softest parts.

He straddled my hips and pinched my nipples, lifting my breasts up, exposing the burning handprints. His tongue traced the hot marks and it was all I could do to keep from scrambling away. Tears slid down my temples and I begged. He ignored me, sucking my nipple into his mouth again and running his tongue over the captive flesh.

"Oh please oh please oh please..."

He released me to grin and I groaned, wanting more, more, more.

"Don't tell me you like this treatment, little slave?"

I shook my head violently, but when he sucked my other nipple into his mouth, the bolt of sensation reached my clit and I groaned with the sheer pleasure of it.

Releasing me, he sat up and shifted forward, his hard cock pressing against my parted lips. I licked them, then tentatively licked the head of his cock.

He smiled at me. "Good girl. Suck me."

I opened my lips, but it was an awkward angle. He leaned forward, propping himself on the headboard, his eyes on mine as his cock sank into my mouth. It reached the back of my throat and I gagged, hot tears slipping out. He pulled back, then started to pump his hips, slowly filling my mouth and retreating. I tried to keep my teeth off his silky flesh, but it was difficult. He pulled out abruptly, settled his knees on either side of my chest.

Jeffery's voice was hoarse. "Pinch your nipples, little slave."

I blinked at him, uncertain, and he reached down to do it for me until I cried out, my hard points throbbing with pain. His hands left, returning to the headboard. "Pinch your nipples."

This time I obeyed, the sensation of gently grasping my own swollen flesh a new wonder for me. He shifted down until his cock lay against my chest, his hairy balls teasing my skin.

"Press your tits together."

I did, awkward, until he showed me where he wanted them, my soft breasts enclosing his cock.

"Hold them there."

My wrists supported the ample flesh, my fingers holding them in place by my nipples. I stayed still, my cunt pulsing with need. Slowly, he pulled back, then thrust forward.

"Does my little slave like it when I fuck her tits?"

His words increased the throb in my cunt and I whimpered in assent.

"Good." He continued thrusting, my saliva providing the lubrication. The jiggling caused my breasts to pull against my fingers, and every time I increased the pressure to keep them still, pleasure spiked through my body. He pulled out and rammed it down my throat again, rewetting it.

"Suck it, slave."

I obeyed as best as I could, drool pooling in my mouth before he withdrew, fucking my tits again. I found I missed the sensation of his cock in my mouth, and I dropped my chin. It was so close, so tempting, the thick red head of his cock appearing and disappearing between my soft mounds. I reached for it with my tongue, and he gasped in surprise. Gratified beyond reason, I grinned, and kept my tongue out, so every thrust pressed his head against it. He groaned, his eyes closing. I watched his abdominal muscles flex and stretch as he sped up, fucking my tits in a frenzy. I closed my eyes, lost in the sensations. When he came, it startled me, thick ropes of cum spattering over my tongue and cheeks. I licked his head, and he groaned again, his cock twitching and pulsing. When he was finished, he withdrew, lying down beside me, his voice in my ear again.

"Clean your face off, Nanette."

I did as he bade, wiping up his hot cum with my fingers and sucking them. He smiled at me.

"Good girl."

Gratified, I wiggled closer, my body practically vibrating with need. "Please, sir?"

He chuckled, his fingers finding their way between my legs again. "I think my good little slave has wet the bed." I flushed to the roots of my hair. He pushed my legs apart again, and I spread them eagerly. He filled me up, three fingers stretching my cunt wide.

"Lift your knees up."

I obeyed, my right foot tucked around behind his back. He slid in slowly, far too slowly for my liking.

"Pinch your nipples again."

I reached for them, biting my lip as my fingers closed over the thick tips.

"Pinch them harder."

I whimpered, and squeezed, the pleasure spiking down to my neglected clit. He slid in and out faster. I groaned. Faster and faster he fucked me, and my fingers loosened, my whole body flopping in lax pleasure.

"No." He stopped abruptly, and I realized my fingers had slipped off my nipples. "Pinch again." I hurriedly obeyed, my cunt throbbing with desperation. "Harder." I pinched until it hurt, whimpering against the pain. "Harder, little slave."

I pinched until tears sprang to my eyes and I mewed. "Good girl. Keep them tight." I whimpered, and his fingers filled me up again. The pain shifted into pleasure as he fucked me. This time he didn't stop, just sent chills through my body with each hot whisper. "Harder." A few more deep thrusts. "Twist them." More thrusting. "Back and forth. Roll them between your fingers." Thrusting. "No. Don't let go. Keep twisting." My breath came in quick gasps and my hips lifted off the bed, tipping towards his big hand, wanting him as deep as possible. "Pinch them again." His fingers, slamming hard into me. "Harder." I didn't think I could handle any more – not another second, not another moment. "Pinch your nipples as hard as you can, little slave, and cum for me." His fingers, ramming into my cunt, the radiating pain from my nipples as I blindly obeyed – it all clashed together and exploded out of my body in hoarse screams of pleasure. I pinched, and kept pinching as hard as I could until the orgasm robbed the strength from my muscles and I collapsed on the bed, completely limp. His fingers were still buried inside me, and I twitched, my cunt squeezing and releasing, grasping and greedy for more.

They were still there when I woke up again. He had tucked me closer to his body, his hard muscles hot against my skin, my breasts aching. His stubble brushed my jaw as his voice sounded in my ear again. "I think my little slave enjoys this." His fingers spread, stretching my oversensitive cunt and I jerked in his hold, my arousal level shooting up again.

"Yes. Please. Yes, sir."

He kissed my jaw, and I longed to feel his lips on my own. I turned towards him, but he tipped his head away.

"No, little slave."

I pouted, hurt that he didn't want to kiss me. His fingers spread again, and I forgot everything except the throbbing in my cunt.

"Please?"

He chuckled. "I have work to do today."

"But, sir?"

"What?"

"How will I function like this?"

He grinned at me, that cruel light back in his eyes. "You'll figure it out or you'll get a good hard spanking tonight." Unbidden, his words did more to arouse me and I shivered. His fingers slid out and I gasped, squirming with need. I reached for my nub, desperate to soothe the need, but he stopped me, rolling me onto my belly, my hands trapped under my body. He spanked me hard, a dozen times on each cheek. It stung, and brought the soreness back to the forefront. "That's just a taste of what you will get if you masturbate. Your pleasure comes from my hand or not at all, little slave."

I shivered, my bottom aching, my breasts aching, my cunt so slippery with desire I couldn't think. He spanked me again, this time on my thighs, and I cried, hot tears of pain mingling with frustration. "Do you understand?"

"Yes, sir! Yes, sir! I'll be good! Just please, please let me cum."

He spread my legs and I whimpered with happiness, relaxing onto the bed. One hand spread my swollen lips and I purred, anticipating pleasure. His hard finger flicked my clit twice and I cried out.

"No."

This time I wept. He got out of bed, washing himself from a small basin in the corner before dressing. I watched him through tear fogged eyes, and then his big hand crashed into my bottom again. "Up. You have work to do."

Reluctant, I dragged my body out of bed and stood before him, wobbling. He pointed at the pitcher of water, the jar of tiny soaps. "Wash."

I started to cry again, but he was implacable. The rough cloth and tepid water did nothing to alleviate my arousal, instead exciting it to a fever pitch. He dumped the soapy water and filled it again. "Rinse again." I wanted to hit him. I even considered it, for one long moment before he caught me about the waist and bent me over, his hard hand landing a half-dozen more times on my sore bottom. "Now." I straightened up when he released me and obeyed.

CHAPTER
SEVEN

JEFFERY LEFT. I stood in the bedroom, staring at the rumpled bed and wondering if any pleasure I could gain from my fingers would be worth the spanking it would earn me.

Jacqueline found me still there, naked, because I was afraid to put my clothes back on, afraid they would further inflame me.

"Oh. Good. Here." She handed me a bundle of cloth, and I realized it was a clean dress, a slightly different shade of blue than the one I'd worn yesterday. Embarrassed, I quickly folded each strip, tying the knot in the middle and draping it around my body, clipping the chain to hold it in place. As predicted, the linen scraped my swollen nipples, scratched my raw buttocks. The sound in my throat must have been audible, because Jacqueline looked at me curiously.

"Did he whip you?"

I cleared my throat. "No. He... spanked me."

"Oh. May I see?"

I hesitated, unsure what Jeffery would prefer me to do. I wanted to commiserate – but Jacqueline seemed to have her own problems. "If – if you like."

Without a word, she walked around behind me and lifted the cloth, tucking it under the chain belt so she could run cool hands over my skin. I flinched, the simmering arousal making even a casual touch into something more than it was. "Does it hurt?"

"Yes."

"Would you like a cream? I have one my Mistress gave me. It helps your skin heal faster."

I bit my lip. Was such a thing allowed? "I don't know. I don't want to anger Jeffery."

She nodded. "That's a wise answer. Disobeying is never a good idea." She patted my bottom gently. "Ask him, next time. If he allows it, let me know."

"Thank you."

She untucked the fabric from the belt, smoothing it back down on my skin and I swallowed hard. She looked at me curiously. "Are you in pain elsewhere?"

I flushed red. "A little."

"Where?"

"My nipples hurt."

She nodded wisely. "Oh, yes. They will, often. Jeffery has a particular fascination for tits."

"Oh? How do you know?"

She half-shrugged. "I've been in his bed often enough."

"Really?" My heart rate increased, but I wasn't sure if it was excitement or distress.

"I'm sure you'll be offered to the other men at some point."

"I will?" My heart hurt – I had thought I was more than a whore to him, special enough to belong to only him.

"Maybe. You remember who you belong to."

"I belong to Jeffery." My chin lifted.

"No." Her tone was gentle, but firm. "You belong to Roy. He allows Jeffery to keep you close, but it's Roy's collar you wear."

I touched the padlock, remembering the ring of little keys on Roy's belt. "I don't want to belong to Roy."

Her full mouth lifted into a sardonic grin. "You don't have much choice in the matter." She gestured impatiently. "Come. You are supposed to help me today."

I let her take my hand and followed her to the kitchen where Lauren was dishing up bowls of porridge. She set one for each of us on a tray, along with another two, spoons stuck in each. One was thin, with the fruit minced fine. I wondered whom it was for, but didn't have time to ask. I caught a quick glimpse of Jeffery speaking to Devon, and then the latter chuckled, looking in my direction. My cheeks flamed, but Jacqueline was leading me quickly towards the stairs.

I looked around curiously at the top of the stairs. It looked similar to the first floor, but there were fewer doors off the hallway. Jacqueline entered one without knocking, then sank gracefully to her knees.

"My lord."

Roy didn't look up. He was slumped in a large chair, dark drapes over the window behind him. Beside him was a massive bed that seemed to dwarf the figure lying in the middle of it. I knelt also, trying to keep the tray steady. When he didn't answer, I took the liberty of looking around the room. It was furnished similarly to the other rooms in the building – a wardrobe, a few chests – but it also held several bookcases and two desks. It had to be at least twice the size of Jeffery's room, if not more. There were more of the massive hooks on the wall here than in his room, and one of the strange pieces of furniture from the dungeon.

Finally my gaze settled back onto the figure on the bed. For a long moment, I wasn't sure it was breathing. Then a hand moved, and her head turned towards us.

The voice was thin, barely audible. "Jackie? Is that you, love?"

Jacqueline trembled, and her voice sparkled with tears. "Yes, Mistress."

Mistress? She rose, and walked to the bedside, sitting carefully on the edge. She waved me in and I followed, setting the tray on a table beside the bed. Roy's eyes followed me, sunken with grief.

"Sit up, my lady. I've got breakfast for you."

The woman on the bed laughed, more breath than sound. "Help me, love."

So Jacqueline wrapped her arms around the woman and lifted her, as if she weighed no more than a feather. I wasn't sure she did. I pulled the pillows up, giving her something soft to lean on. Jacqueline let her relax down.

"Here."

Tenderly, Jacqueline spooned the thin porridge up and began to feed the woman. A pale ghost of her former self, I could see the lines of her bones, how irresistible she must have been in life. Even now, I could feel the pull of her spirit. Jacqueline was occupied with the woman on the bed, and I stood there helpless, unsure how I was supposed to help. I glanced again at Roy. He had made no move towards the food.

I set my chin. If I belonged to him, it was my responsibility to make sure he kept up his strength. A man couldn't protect much if he wasted away while his – wife? slave? lover? - did. I picked up the largest bowl of porridge, the one piled high with fruits and nuts, then walked around the bed and knelt in front of him. Remembering the way Jacqueline had addressed him, I raised my eyes to his.

"Please, my lord. Here is your breakfast." He ignored me. I set it down on the table beside him, and stood in front of him. He turned towards the bed. The frail woman fluttered a hand, and Jacqueline stopped the spoon.

It was difficult to make out her words. "Roy. You have to."

"No, Jessica, I don't. I am governor here."

I placed a hand on each of his bearded cheeks and he turned to me, frowning.

"My lord. Do you protect your own?"

There was anger behind his voice. "Of course, slave."

"I am one of your own."

"Of course." He flicked the padlock on my collar, the movement reminding me of the way Jeffery flicked my clit, and I shivered, my eyes rolling back momentarily. It struck his curiosity, and he actually looked at me for the first time. "You're Nanette."

"Yes, sir."

"What are you doing here?"

"I'm bringing you food."

He flicked his fingers dismissively. "Take it back. I don't want it."

"No."

He looked at me again, eyebrows raised. "What did you say to me?"

I could hear Jacqueline gasp behind me, and I bit my lip, knowing I was treading on dangerous ground.

"I said no. I am not taking it back. Not until that bowl is empty."

I could feel his anger rising. "Insolent little mouth." He caught my hair and pushed me to my knees, out of his sight. In that position, it reminded me of Jeffery's ungentle attentions.

"You can punish my insolent mouth later, as long as you eat first." I wasn't even sure where my daring came from. Something about watching a powerful man crumble plucked at my self-preservation.

Surprising me, he laughed. It was a rusty sound, harsh and unfunny. But it was a laugh.

"You are a terrible brat, aren't you?"

"No, sir."

"No?" he laughed again. I could feel the atmosphere lighten. "What is this, if not a bratty mouth?" His fingers were harsh on my lips, so I kissed them.

"It's a smart mouth."

He slapped me gently, barely raising a sting on my cheek. "That's the same thing."

"No, sir. I say smart things, true things, even if you don't like them. I'm not a brat for no reason." His hand softened on my face, and I leaned into it. "That's Stephanie's job, isn't it?"

I remembered her cold smile and nasty laugh.

"Probably."

I realized he'd done a lot of talking, but no eating. "My lord. Your porridge?"

He sighed, and picked up the bowl. I watched carefully until he'd taken several large bites, and then I couldn't help myself. "Good boy."

He coughed, his face turning red. I heard Jacqueline desperately covering her snorting, and the soft breathy laughter that was Jessica's. I suddenly wondered about my sanity as he set the bowl down and his hand wrapped around the back of my neck. I went without hesitation, anxiety flaring as I wondered if I'd just gone way too far in my prodding.

I had. He tucked me down over his right knee and pulled the two rear strips of my dress to opposite sides, baring my sore bottom. His voice held a trace of laughter when he spoke, and I wasn't sure if I should be reassured or more concerned.

"Jacqueline, hand me the tawse."

I squirmed at the unfamiliar word, twisting to try to see what it was. Once I'd seen, I wished I hadn't. It had a long handle and a thick flat tail that was split in two places, making three strips of leather. It cracked across my bottom and I shrieked, gasping at the unbelievable pain. A line of fire burned its way to my core and I squirmed frantically. He tucked my legs under his left thigh and shifted me forward until my nose nearly bumped the floor. Another crack and my hands flew back, covering my bottom and trying to rub away the pain. He caught my wrists easily and tucked them against the small of my back, pressing in until I arched, tipping my bottom higher for him. Another two cracks and I wailed, wishing I had kept my stupid mouth shut. The next crack landed across the crease between buttock and thigh and I began to cry. A final crack across the back of my thighs and he released me, pushing me back down to the floor. I knelt up, afraid to sit with the throbbing in my bottom.

I felt a hand on my hair, and I turned, sniffling. Jessica caressed my face with a delicate finger. "Such a good girl."

I sniffled some more, not feeling much like a good girl. "Thank you, my lady."

It wasn't until I saw the awe and pride in Jacqueline's face that I realized the sound behind me was the scrape of Roy's spoon in his bowl. I stayed where I was, my head resting on the bed, Jessica's finger on my face, until Roy's words roused me. "Get up."

I did, standing before him with my hands clasped penitently. "I'm sorry, my lord."

He snorted, but it was laughter. "Don't be. Thank you." He handed me the empty bowl, and I saw a faint glimmer of something a bit like determination in his eyes.

"You're welcome, my lord."

I took the bowl, and Jacqueline looked up. "Go ahead and take it back to the kitchen with your own. I'll stay here with Jessica." I nodded, leaving the tray with Jacqueline's bowl on it where it was, and slipped out the door.

Each step going down the stairs hurt. There was no one left in the dining room, and Lauren was alone in the kitchen. She look a look at the bowls and then my face before taking them out of my hands and spinning me around. I protested, but she pushed me over a chair and lifted my dress.

"Please, no! Please, ma'am, he already punished me, please, please, please don't spank me again."

"Shush, girl. I'm not going to spank you. I just want to see why you're moving so stiffly."

I settled down, my face still flushed with embarrassment. Her fingers were light on my welts. "What did you do?"

"I called him a good boy."

She barked out a laugh. "And he only gave you six?"

I nodded. "He was... amused."

She shook her head and pulled out a jar. Scooping out a dollop, she dropped it in my palm. It smelled vaguely sweet and bitter, medicinal.

"Rub that in." I thought about asking if Jeffery would mind, then reminded myself he'd told me to obey her. Surely he couldn't be angry if she told me to do it. So I stood up, rubbing my palms together and then smoothing it over my raw skin. I traced the puffy lines with my fingers, awed by how much they hurt.

"Try to not sit down."

I nodded, adjusting my dress panels to cover my buttocks again, and wiped my hands with a cloth she held out.

"What's wrong with Jessica?"

She shrugged, her face closed. "Some sort of disease. No one knows exactly what it is, but she's getting weaker by the day. She won't last much longer."

"Who is she?"

"She's his queen. The love of his life. His first, perfect slave. His partner." She shrugged. "She's the one who's been with him since the beginning, since he was a boy and she was a girl and they wanted to find a way to protect their friends, a way to combine forces and carve out a little oasis in this dangerous world."

"Jacqueline called her Mistress."

"And so she is. Mistress of Brackish Bay, the Lady of the House. Jacqueline belongs to her. Stephanie is her lover, as are Roy's inner circle, the Ward brothers and the Herring brothers."

"Jeffery is her lover?" My voice seemed to rise a little.

"Yes, of course."

I blinked, startled. "He never mentioned it."

Lauren snorted. "And? You're his slave. You expect him to tell you everything?"

I blinked again, wondering. Did I expect him to tell me everything that was going on in the house, about all the relationships between the people? I did, actually, expect that. And it didn't seem unreasonable, no matter what Lauren thought of it. If I was going to throw my lot in with the House of Brackish Bay, I expected to be informed. I made up my mind to talk to Jeffery when he returned.

She broke into my thoughts. "Eat before it's completely cold."

I remained standing while I obeyed.

The rest of the morning was spent finishing the canning that Lauren had started the day before, and cooking dinner for everyone, including a number of additional men and women who were working on the island that day. Jeffery came into the kitchen just as we were finishing and surprised me with a hand under my skirts. I squealed, and Lauren scolded him sharply. He apologized for intruding, then picked me up and bumped my back into the nearest clear wall, my legs wrapped tight around his waist, my arms around his neck.

"Oh!"

He grinned at me, a wicked light in his eyes. "How much did you miss me, little slave?"

My arousal had finally faded as I concentrated on other things, but feeling his hard cock through his pants, pressing tight against my sopping slit, brought it all back in a rush. I moaned softly. "A lot."

"Good girl."

I tipped my face up, hoping for a kiss, but he just smiled that cruel smile and lazily ground his pelvis into mine. His fingers dug into my buttocks and I winced, which only widened his smile. He leaned forward, resting his forehead on the wall behind my head, his hot whispers in my ear. "I expect you to serve me well tonight before you get any relief. I want to feel your tongue on my cock. And I want your poor empty cunt to drip down your thighs all day, just thinking about how much you want to suck me. How much you want to feel my fingers inside you."

I squirmed against him, every movement inflaming my arousal. My nipples were so hard I was afraid they'd wear through my dress. He put me down, and I stumbled, holding tightly to his clothes to steady myself. His hands spanned my waist, and I felt small, vulnerable. He reached up then and pinched my nipples hard. I gasped, my hands covering my breasts protectively as I hunched over. My clit pulsed with need.

A thick finger under my chin directed me to straighten up. "Are you hiding your tits from me?" His voice was amused. "Up."

I straightened my spine, lifting my chin at the pressure from his finger. "Hands down."

I clenched my jaw, swallowing hard, and slowly lowered my hands. Pressing them flat to my hips, I took a deep breath.

"Shoulders back. Didn't your father ever teach you how to stand up straight?"

He had, and I found myself shifting into better posture at his words. It left my breasts exposed and vulnerable. The tips throbbed, crinkled and tight with pain and pleasure. He cupped my breasts then, his thumbs rubbing back and forth over my nubs until I shuddered. His forefingers slid closer and closer. My chest heaved with the effort of staying still while he played. He pinched then, gently, twisting until my head fell back against the wall and I groaned aloud, no longer caring who might hear me in the dining room. Abruptly he released me, and I stumbled back a step, bracing myself against the wall. He leaned in and nipped my earlobe. "Good little slave." And then he was gone.

Lauren stared after him, her arms folded and a scowl on her face. "Jeffrey! What am I going to do now? She's useless like that." He must have said something flippant, because she cursed under her breath. I took a deep breath, and attempted to stand up. My legs wobbled but I made it.

"I can help."

She eyed me critically. "Start carrying the food out to the table. I'll put it on the counter in order of seating, starting with Roy."

"Yes, ma'am." My limbs were weak with want, but didn't want to seem completely useless. So I steadied each plate with both hands, and took one at a time to the table. Jeffery patted my aching bottom every time I passed him, which didn't help matters at all. Finally everyone had been served, and I thought I could escape to the kitchen – but it was not to be. He snapped his fingers and pointed at the floor. I bit my lip, whining softly, but he raised an eyebrow and I went. Kneeling at his feet while he ate and conversed was no less humiliating than it had been the night before, and quite a bit worse given the thrumming of excitement in my blood and the lack of other slaves present. Lauren brought my plate to him, and he placed it on the floor, but this time didn't give me a spoon. I nearly cried.

A hand in my hair pushed me towards it, so I gave up and leaned forward. It was a variety of fried fish and vegetables on top of rice. I glanced up. He wasn't watching. I picked up the fish with my fingers and ate it. The one benefit of being alone under the table was that there was no one to tattle on me. I smiled to myself and ate quickly, careful to block the view of my plate with my shoulder, just in case he glanced down, and keeping my head low, so it wouldn't be obvious I wasn't eating like a dog. Though why that pleased him, I had no idea. It was incredibly humiliating. Still, the food was delicious, as was everything that Lauren touched. The spice was just right, the breading fatty and crisp but not soggy. I filled my stomach, pleased that the vegetables I'd cut for her had fried up so well.

After a bit, I paused. Nothing was left but the rice on my plate, and that would be difficult to eat with my fingers. Not that I couldn't do it. But if I did, it would be harder to hide it. Rice was sticky – I couldn't just lick my fingers and hide them if he looked down. I thought about trying to eat like a dog, and found the idea unpleasant. Glancing upwards again, he seemed to be discussing something about moving some of the house's big nets from one side of the river to another. That ought to take a bit of time. I scooped up rice in my fingers and shoveled it in my mouth. It was beyond good, having been cooked in fish broth and having soaked up the dipping sauce served with the vegetables. But it was very sticky. Juice ran down my chin and my fingers stuck together. I continued to eat, hoping to finish before he wanted my attention.

It wasn't to be so. He leaned down and tugged on a lock of my hair, and I straightened up, bumping my head again. I winced. When would I learn? Scooting back out, I looked up. He glanced down and started to laugh at me. I flushed, humiliated, as he called for a wet cloth, still laughing. When Lauren brought it, I could see even her smirking at my appearance. My face got hot, and I hung my head, but he was having none of it. Cloth in hand he tipped my face back then washed me before handing it to me. "Wash your fingers." I obeyed, glancing longingly at the last bit of food in my bowl.

My voice rose in a soft plea. "Spoon?"

He raised an eyebrow, then relented, handing me his spoon. I could tell he'd used it, and suddenly the idea of licking the same spoon he had was very erotic. Given that he'd not kissed me, we'd not exchanged saliva at all. I stuck the spoon in my mouth and ran my tongue over it, wondering if I'd finally lost all sense. The rice called to me, so I finished eating, the damp cloth firmly in hand for any mishaps. There were none, and I finally knelt up, resting my head against his thigh while he petted me absently and I idly sucked on the spoon.

CHAPTER
EIGHT

WHEN EVERYONE WAS FINISHED with dinner, he took the spoon out of my mouth and set in on his plate to carry back to the kitchen. I piled his and mine together and took them out, then cleared the rest of the table. Various people thanked me as they were leaving, and I was gratified that my work did not go unnoticed. When I reached Devon's place, he caught me about the waist and pulled me down into his lap. I glanced in alarm at Jeffery, but he grinned at me. Flustered, I struggled a little, but Devon tucked me against his chest.

"Shush, Nanette. I won't harm you."

I tried to relax, but my body was so sensitive the feel of his rough clothing on my skin caused me to squirm shamefully. He pressed his lips to my temple and I froze.

His voice was in my ear, so quiet the others exiting wouldn't hear him. "Have you been a good little slave for my brother?"

I nodded slowly, glancing to Jeffery for confirmation. He leaned back in his chair, the predatory grin on his face again. "Would you also be a good little slave for me?"

I pushed away from him. "Only if he says so."

Jeffery's eyes were sparkling. "Good girl, Nanette."

I risked another glance at him.

"Come here."

I rose, glad that Devon released me – there would have been no way I could escape otherwise. He pointed to the floor, and I sank down to the cushion. He caressed my hair, then leaned forward.

"I might share you with my brother, if you are a good little slave." Despite myself, despite my earlier distaste at the idea, I felt my body ripen. The idea of two such cocks as Jeffery's, filling and thrusting inside me was intoxicating.

"Yes, sir."

He caressed my cheek, and they rose, leaving me alone on the cushion, dazed and desiring.

Lauren came in then, washing the table and nudging me with her foot. "Get up. You still have plenty to work on before you can play." I heaved a sigh, and got to my feet.

The afternoon was spent in cleaning the dungeon. I wondered if it was Lauren's way of adding to Jeffery's torment, or if she was simply unaffected.

The furniture was strange. There was an X shape, with big loops of metal at the end of each bar, and additional chains hanging. There was a lowercase T shape, also with big loops of metal at the end of each bar. There was a funny sort of bench with smaller, lower bars of padding on either side of a broad one. There was a large rectangular frame, with many metal hooks and loops, and a large variety of chains hanging off it. There was a triangular frame, three beams coming together in a point, also with loops and chains. Several regular benches and chairs, and a couple chests full of blankets and pillows. One wall was covered with implements of corporal punishment, and this is what she told me to clean first.

"Take each one down. Clean it, polish it, return it to its hook."

I started at one side of the room, fingering each item with a raw fascination. I'd never seen anything like these items. Daddy had spanked Suzanna and me, true, but only with his hand, and gently at that. These were vicious. Designed to punish thoroughly, they were heavy, or thick, or broad; stiff or flexible, all of them sent a shiver down my spine. I came to a tawse similar to the one Roy had used, and bit my lip as I wiped it down. My bottom throbbed as I imagined what each one might feel like on my skin. At the far end were long whips that struck terror into my heart. *Did he whip you?* Jacqueline had inquired, as if it were a definite possibility. I prayed that I would never know what they felt like. Silently, I pleaded with the goddess. *Eris, please help me please him so well that he never sees need to whip me.*

That done, Lauren directed me to the walls and I had to handle each item again to wash the wall. She provided me with a long handled mop to clean the highest portion of the walls. I finished by the time she had finished washing down all of the furniture. "Floor," she said, leaving me with a fresh bucket and rags. I tied up my skirts and started in the far corner. It was nearly ten times the size of the bathroom, and took me considerably longer. By the time I finished, my shoulders were aching, my back was aching, and my buttocks was, of course, still aching. My knees were bruised, and my nipples were raw from chafing on the linen of my dress. I brushed my hair out of my face, kneeling up in the hallway. Surveyed the gleaming dungeon, I nodded to myself.

After a long moment I felt eyes on me, and turned slowly. Roy was standing in the hallway watching me silently.

"Yes, sir?" I was glad my voice didn't shake. Much.

"You're a hard worker."

I nodded. "Yes, sir. My sister and I were raised to do whatever needed to be done."

"Raised by whom?"

"Our father and mother."

"Why are you not still with them?"

I looked away, and he let me take the time I needed to gather my voice. "We were attacked." He waited. "My father is a fisherman. He taught us how to fish as soon as we could hold a net. He caught plenty extra, and sold them to people in the nearby village. We lived out in the forest, by the river where he worked." He let the silence stretch out. "I don't know why. I'm not sure who. I just know that he saw them coming, and he told us to run, to escape before they saw us. We were supposed to go to Torrent and wait for him and Mom to find us there." I wiped away my tears. "He said if they didn't find us in a year, they were probably dead." I sniffled. "I messed up. I couldn't find Caladonia. I found Solon all right, but I couldn't find Caladonia. I don't know if I could find Torrent."

He was frowning. "Caladonia burned to the ground a year ago. Someone tried to work out electricity, tried to wire the whole place. They even got a small power plant running again. But something went wrong, either in the wiring or something else, and the whole place went up in flames and invisible death. It's a good thing you didn't find it. I've heard some of the wires are still live, can still kill through the water."

I blanched. "What about Torrent?"

"Torrent is upriver from us. A few weeks hike at most."

My eyes widened. "Could we go?"

He shook his head. "No. Between them and us is Ken's Corner, and he's dangerous. If he caught you in his territory, you would not live long. He and his men use women up like rag dolls."

I hung my head, defeated, until a sudden thought struck me. "Could we send word, to the man we were supposed to meet there? So if he sees them, he can tell them where we are?"

Roy seemed thoughtful. Then he nodded. "The next time my men travel there, I'll have them deliver a message."

I beamed at him. "Thank you!"

He smiled slightly. "Are you satisfied that I and my House mean you and your sister no harm?"

I thought about it. I'd experienced pain many times at his hand and those of his men. But harmed? I didn't think we'd been harmed. He seemed to be far more honorable than, for example, those of Ken's Corner. Or the men who had attacked our parents, for that matter. "What will happen to my sister if we stay here?"

He hunkered down, leaning against the wall and watching me. "She will grow up with Marcus and Julia's children. When she's a woman grown, she'll be allowed to chose a husband from the men available and interested."

"What men?"

"My men. I have five stations, two on either side of the river where it broadens on its way to the sea. One here, on the island with us. All of my men are absolutely loyal, absolutely honorable. Any who are not are killed or sold."

I sucked in a breath. This man was even more powerful than most of the warlords I'd heard of growing up. It was even more imperative that he keep functioning, despite his woman's slow death. My heart ached for him.

"And if there are none suitable?"

"She'll be bound into slavery and offered to what man as has earned such a reward."

"Like me?"

He nodded. "Like you."

I did not want Suzanna to become a slave. But if he had as many men as he said he did – and I remembered the number of voices on the dock when we arrived, the people who'd come in for supper the day before and dinner today, the men I saw out the windows patrolling. There were probably many eligible bachelors.

"What did Jeffery do to earn me?"

"He has been loyal to me for a long time. He and Devon run the fishing in the Bay. He's never asked to keep a woman before, not any of the ones we've found in our territory, not any of the grown daughters. There was just something about you."

I blushed, warmed and heartened. His eyes softened and he caressed my cheek.

"You're good for this House, Nanette. I hope you come to consider this your home."

I looked down, unsure how to answer. For a long moment we stayed silent, contemplating the cruelties of the world. *Eris*, I begged wordlessly, *if you would, heal Jessica. Protect Daddy and Mom. Watch over Suzanna.* Nothing answered but a silent echo of my thoughts.

Lauren found us there in the hallway. Her voice was gentle. "Come to supper, Roy." He glanced at me and I put on my best stern face, wagging my finger at him. Lauren snorted. "I wouldn't do that so close to the dungeon if I were you." I froze mid-wag, glancing involuntarily inside the room. Roy actually grinned then, and my mouth rounded into an O of consternation.

"Come." He held out a hand to me and helped me stand. "I'm too hungry to bother spanking you now."

I shivered, my hand still wrapped in his big one, and swallowed hard, glancing at him under my lashes. He was a rugged man. His hair was dark and short, his muscles heavy and veined. A long scar ran across his jaw and continued down the middle of his neck. I wondered what – or who – had caused it, and decided I was very glad that my teasing had not angered him.

We entered the dining room together, and it was just the inner circle of men again. Tobin had Stephanie's hair in a fist as she knelt at his knee, and Jeffrey had moved my cushion so it was between his and Devon's chair. My pulse beat harder at the implication. Roy led me to it and released me. I sank down, embarrassed to realize I'd still had the skirts tied up around my thighs. I untied it while Lauren brought out the plates.

The food was a thick stew, and no amount of making eyes at Jeffery would convince him to hand me a spoon this time, so I hunkered down, trying to figure out the best way to eat it. Stephanie had tucked her wrists under the rim of the plate, tipping it up slightly, then biting and licking the food out of the side closest to her. She ignored me. I attempted to imitate her, but accidentally spilled some. Chagrined, I resorted to picking out the chunks with my fingers. The fish was tender and the roots were deliciously mealy, but both tended to fall apart when grasped. Eating supper like a pet was an exercise in frustration. It was made even more difficult by Devon's tendency to reach down and pinch my aching bottom now and again.

When it was over, Jeffery handed me a damp cloth to wash with, and I cleaned the floor before taking my plate to the kitchen. I had just started to wash the dishes when Jeffery appeared in the doorway.

"Come, Nanette," he said, and Lauren shooed me away from the sink.

I followed him to his room, Devon following close behind. Jeffery gestured at me. "Strip."

I obeyed, and the men left. Biting my lip I waited, and finally they returned, lugging one of the tubs. It was filled with steaming water. When it had been set on the floor, Jeffery pointed. "In."

I obeyed, sighing. The hot water felt so very good on my aching body. I reached for the washcloth on the handle, but Devon took it from me.

"My turn."

His ministrations were faster than Jeffery's had been the first morning, but more arousing, given my day of teasing. I moaned, arching into his hand when he washed my breasts. When his hand found the swollen nub between my nether lips and pinched it, I jerked, splashing water out of the tub and crying out. Jeffery knelt behind me and pinched my raw nipples, dipping his head to whisper in my ear.

"I hear you've been a good little slave today."

"Yes, sir!"

"Even Roy said so, despite having to punish you."

I warmed up, pleased beyond expectation that he said it, hot for Jeffery's rough ministrations. "Yes, sir!"

"But you still have a few more things to do before you get any relief."

I whimpered. "Sir?"

"You have to suck me. And you have to suck Devon." I squirmed, caught between their pinching fingers. The thought of two cocks down my throat ignited something in my core.

"Yes, sir!"

He grinned that cruel smile, and stood up. Devon pinched hard on my clit; I jerked when he released me.

"Out." I obeyed, and Jeffrey wrapped me in a towel before stripping and getting in the hot bath. I stood adrift, watching his hard muscles as he scrubbed himself efficiently. When he was finished, he knelt up, lazily stroking his hard cock and watching my expression. I bit my lip, unable to look away, unable to do anything but fantasize about his thickness inside me. He got out, and Devon got in. I watched him next, comparing him to his brother. He was a little shorter, but their shoulders were equally broad. His hair was a shade darker, but his cock was just as thick and long, his balls just as heavy. I found my mouth filling with saliva at the thought of his hands in my hair.

As I watched, Jeffery finished drying himself and slid a hand up the back of my neck, tightening in my hair. His left arm wrapped around my waist and his lips teased my ear as he spoke. "You belong to me. Devon doesn't get to use any of your holes except your smart mouth. You will be a good little slave and please him, won't you?"

I squirmed, both at the thought of Devon's cock in my mouth, and Jeffery's cock elsewhere. He bit the juncture of my neck and my shoulder and I gasped, my hands lifting to push him away, then hovering, helpless, as he ignored my protest.

Devon was out of the tub now. He watched me with half-closed eyes as he stroked his hard length. "Ready, Nanette?"

I nodded, and Jeffery pushed me to my knees. I looked up to see Devon watching me, then opened my mouth for him. He placed the tip of his cock on my tongue, then stood still, his hands behind his back.

"Please me."

I hesitated, uncertain what he would like, but when he simply waited, I licked the smooth head. Bolder, I licked down his shaft to his hair, then back again. Feeling a bit like a cat with cream, I covered his cock in teasing licks.

"Don't forget my balls."

I shifted lower, licking his hairy balls until they were glistening with my saliva. He widened his stance so I could reach better, and I laved him thoroughly, from perineum to seeping hole.

I felt Jeffery kneel down behind me, and I anticipated his fingers on my nipples. I did not anticipate the sharp bite of something cold and hard. I yelped, jerking away from Devon and looked down. Clamps were fastened on my nipples, a chain dangling between them. The jaws were cruel on my thick nipples and I whimpered, eyes watering. Jeffery's hands lifted my heavy breasts, jiggling them so that the chain tugged on the clamps. I whimpered. His gravely voice whispered in my ear. "Keep sucking."

Reaching for Devon, I wrapped my hands around his hips to brace myself, and took his cock inside my mouth. On my own, I could only take it about two thirds of the way down, sucking and licking as I bobbed on his shaft. Jeffery stopped me.

"I want to use your ass."

I froze, eyes flying wide open. Devon stepped away, and Jeffery patted the bed.

"Up here."

I climbed on, the weight on my sore nipples stirring my arousal to fever pitch. Devon stood beside the bed, facing me, and I crawled forward. This time he took my hair in his hands, pulling me down slowly, so very slowly that I had time to relax my throat and swallow him whole. Concentrating on breathing, I forgot momentarily about Jeffery's words, until his knees settled beside mine and I felt his oiled fingers pressing against my bottom hole. "Relax your asshole, little slave."

Something in the way he said it, the tender strictness in his voice, compelled me to obey. So I did. His finger slid in deep, and I moaned around Devon's cock. Devon held my head down until I gagged, my body tensing, my asshole squeezing Jeffery's finger until the sensation radiated through my pelvis. Devon relaxed his grip on my head and I pulled back, sucking in air. Jeffery slid his finger in and out, in and out, stroking my insides and capturing my attention. My cunt felt neglected, empty and grasping, juice flooding my thighs. His finger slid all the way out, and I mewed, wanting.

His oiled cock slid against my crack, and then pressed hard on my asshole. Devon pulled my head forward, brushing my lips with his curly hair, and I swallowed hard, trying not to gag.

"Relax, little slave."

Devon pushed me back, shoving my face down against the bed,

my mouth empty and covered in drool. The position pushed my ass against Jeffery, and he slid in, pressing deep until I was stuffed full and moaning. Being held down, my clamped nipples pressed hard against the bed, my hips caught in Jeffery's big hands – it all wrapped around my core and I cried out, desperate for release. Jeffery began to thrust, his hips banging mine, his heavy balls slapping my sopping cunt lips, teasing my swollen clit. Devon pulled my head back up and rammed his cock down my throat until I gagged, tears streaming out of my eyes. I rocked forward and back, each thrust from one man knocking me into the other.

Jeffery's voice. "Squeeze me hard."

I clenched my asshole, and the pleasure stepped up, increasing with each stroke.

Devon's voice. "Suck me."

I tried to keep suction on his cock, but he thrust hard, banging the back of my throat until I just gave up, reveling in the intensity of every sensation. When I came, it was a wave of feelings too big for my body to contain. I cried out until I was hoarse, my throat vibrating with my groans, my asshole slick and tight. Devon erupted first, shooting hot cum down my throat as I swallowed and sucked, not wanting to lose a drop. He pulled out and I collapsed forward onto the bed, Jeffery still ramming my ass. Devon's hands under my soft breasts released the clamps and rubbed my nipples. Pain shot through my breasts and I came again, bucking against Jeffery's hips. This time he came, his hips sealed tight against my welted bottom as hot cum spurted deep in my bowels.

I didn't remember falling asleep. I did remember waking briefly as Jeffery wiped me down. Lifting me, he tucked me under the sheets, his arms wrapped around me from behind. I slept.

CHAPTER
NINE

MY DAYS STARTED to fall into a routine. I awoke in Jeffery's arms. I had breakfast in the kitchen and worked with Lauren on whatever needed to be done. I ate at Jeffery's feet if he came in for dinner or supper, and in the kitchen if he did not. My heart warred with conflicting wants over meals – as much as I preferred to eat in the kitchen, I began to crave his touch, his presence, with a surety that eclipsed every other desire. The scab of my bite peeled off and it was just a pair of dark pink crescents on his forearm. In the evenings, he took me to his bed and fucked me into oblivion. If Jeffery was feeling generous, Devon helped.

The first day he was gone for the night, it hurt.

He wasn't present for supper, but I had grown accustomed to him coming in late some days, if a net needed extra mending, or there was a greater catch than expected. So I was cleaning the kitchen, waiting to hear his footsteps, when Devon came in.

"Nanette."

I turned, blushing with pleasure at the thought of him playing with us that night.

"Come."

I dried my hands and followed. When we didn't enter Jeffery's room, instead turned into Devon's, I was surprised. He pointed to a cushion and I knelt down, my brows raised.

"Where is Jeffery?"

"He won't be back for the next week, at least. He's taking the batch of brined fish to the village to sell."

I knew that men were sent in with fresh fish every day, but I hadn't known they kept part of their salable catch to preserve.

"Why?"

"There's a lot. One of us always goes with the very big shipments like this. We sell it in lots to the stores, not to individuals like the fresh fish."

"Oh." I continued to kneel, watching him remove his clothing and hang it up, washing himself quickly in the basin. "Where am I supposed to sleep?"

He indicated the bed. "With me."

My heart rate sped up, uncertainty flitting through my thoughts. I wished Jeffery had told me this, not let me discover it myself.

"Do – do you want me to please you, first?" I blushed, my tongue touching the roof of my mouth as I remembered the salty bitter tang of his cock, similar but not quite the same as his brother's.

He sat back on the bed. "Yes."

I crawled to him, my heavy breasts swaying. I knelt up, holding tight to his hairy knees. He caressed my face, running his thumb over my lower lip until I bit it, trying to ease the tingling sensation. He smiled and guided my face down. I began to lick his half-mast cock until it woke up. I grinned, knowing I was the reason it stood at attention. He spread his legs wider, shifting closer to the edge of the bed so I could lick his balls, also. I had found he liked that almost better than my tongue on his shaft, so I'd learned to pay special attention to them.

Intent on my task, his hands on my breasts startled me. Freeing them from the crisscrossing fabric that made up my dress, he fondled them, jumpstarting my own arousal. I moaned around his cock when he pinched the tips, rolling them between his fingers until they swelled. My hair brushed his chest as he hunched over me, flicking his fingers over my thick buds. I sucked harder, eager to swallow his cock. I'd gotten better at breathing around their thrusts, and something about having my face helpless before their onslaught left me dripping wet. Mostly everything they did to me left me dripping wet, and tonight was no exception. By the time he was ready to ram my throat, there was a puddle on the floor. He released my sore nipples, standing to grab my head. I groaned, taking him all the way to the back of my throat, his wiry hair scratching my lips, his flat belly bumping my nose. He spurted, as usual, holding me tight to his hips until he'd finished. I swallowed hard, gasping for air.

He lay back on the bed and I stripped, going to the basin to wash off. Baths were a less frequent luxury. Naked except for the constant chain on my throat, I climbed into bed beside him.

He spoke, his voice a half step higher than his brother's. "I want to try something."

I watched him, eyes wide. He smiled that lazy smile, then reached down to spread my legs. I surrendered, my swollen lips parting, my cunt dripping. His fingers found my clit and I twitched, my nipples crinkling into harder points.

"Hold your thighs open."

I obeyed, my hands pressing down. He ran the palm of his hand over my wet lips, coating the whole of it with my arousal. I moaned. He lifted his hand, and spanked my open lips. I jerked, my legs closing and a cry coming from my lips.

"No. I told you to hold your thighs open. Do it, or I'll spank them too."

I whimpered, then pressed down hard. His wet hand grazed my swollen flesh. I squeezed my eyes shut. That was worse. The slap burned my tender bits and I cried out, my eyes flying open. "Oh! Please! Please no!"

"Shush, little girl."

I took a deep breath, settling back on the bed, but kept my eyes on his arm. He stroked me, spreading my lips for better access to my clit. I closed my eyes, arching back. The slap startled me again, hot and stinging. I moaned, feeling the throb start, pain twisting into pleasure. He slid his hand along my slit again, wetting it thoroughly.

I forced myself to watch, no matter how soothing it was. He raised his hand, and I held my breath. He slapped down, rebounding on my wet skin with a pop. I gasped, panting, the sting nearly too much for me to bear.

"Close your lips for me."

I hesitated until he took my hands and placed them on either side of my swollen cunt lips, pressing them closed. I whimpered, and he spanked my outer lips, a dozen times, until they stung and burned.

"Open them."

I let them part, but he pinched my lips, showing me how he wanted me to hold them, spread wide. I whined, but he ignored me, spanking the inner lips and my clit. I shook, my fingers digging in as my slippery flesh tried to escape my grip. When he was satisfied with the crimson hue of my punished flesh, he stopped. I moaned, completely incoherent. He watched me beg, amused that he could bring me to that.

Finally he took pity on me, and slid a single finger inside my cunt. I clenched, gasping, tipping my hips towards his hand. I found my voice. "More... please! Please! F – fu – fuck me, please!"

"Good girl." He slipped a second finger in, and began to thrust, slowly – far too slowly. I mewed, needing more. He slipped a third in, and I sighed in relief. It didn't help much, not as slowly as he was thrusting.

"Please!"

He chuckled, and swept my thighs up over his shoulder, slamming his fingers in and out, fucking me hard. I keened. He twisted his hand, jamming his thumb against my clit with each thrust and I finally screamed my release. He didn't stop, but forced me up over the peak again, and a third time before I collapsed.

I woke to find my head pillowed on his shoulder, his breath ruffling my hair. My cunt was sore, both from his hard fingers and my desperate clenching. My fingers fluttered over his chest. "Why doesn't Jeffery ever fuck my cunt?"

"He doesn't want to father any children. Not yet. So he doesn't want to risk it."

"Oh." It made perfect sense. My mother had scolded me for that very reason when she'd found out about my explorations with Tommy. But I still wished to feel his hard cock inside me.

"Don't worry, little slave. We'll make sure your cunt gets well used."

I mewed a little, snuggling closer to him. It certainly had been well used tonight.

I SAW SUZANNA AGAIN THE DAY THAT JESSICA DIED. MARCUS AND JULIA brought her with the rest of their daughters to pay their respects to the governor. We didn't speak, just hugged for a long moment before returning to our respective duties. She looked well, though. Modestly clothed, well fed, her face was starting to fill out again from the leanness it had acquired during our long flight.

Roy sat in an armchair someone had brought down from his room and placed in the dining room, the table pushed to the side. He stared at nothing, barely rousing to acknowledge people's condolences. Jacqueline knelt at his feet, her tears a steady drip down his pants. Stephanie knelt on his other side, distressed and restless. Tobin and Gerard waited on him, bringing him drinks, or food, directing the people who came in, thanking them and sending them on their way.

I stayed in the kitchen, helping Lauren. There were a half a dozen other slaves, brought in by the men who kept them and left to make themselves useful. Devon was conspicuous by his absence. I found out later he had taken it upon himself to direct all of the House's business for a few days – the fishing, the farming, the patrolling – so Tobin and Gerard could focus on Roy.

All of us wore white. Old dresses or pants or shirts, bleached bone white in the sun. I missed Jeffery dreadfully, and Devon also. Sleeping on a mat on the kitchen floor with the other slaves left me anxious and lonely. They all seemed to know each other, and whispered together often.

The brunette. "Do you think he'll take another slave?"

The one with braids. "No way. Jessica was his life. No one could possibly compare."

The dark one. "But he has the rest of us. Surely someone is good enough to warm his bed?"

Braids again. "Warm his bed – sure. Take her place? No way in hell."

The brunette. "She was very sweet. I didn't know her well, but she was really sweet."

A blonde streaked with gray. "She was a true Lady. It won't be the same without her."

The dark one turned towards me. "Have you been with our lord yet?"

I shook my head.

"Why not?"

I shrugged. "I don't think he has had interest in anyone for a long time."

They considered that. The gray-blonde spoke up. "That makes sense. I've heard Stephanie has been a downright surly bitch lately, and he used to be one of the best at keeping her in line. I bet he hasn't done anything with anyone since the doctor told him Jessica wasn't getting better."

A red head. "He must have loved her an awful lot."

Braids. "He loved her more than the world. This – this whole thing, his territory – this was her idea."

The dark one. "Really? Why?"

Braids. "She wanted there to be a place that was safe for men and women. In the wide world, a woman or child is only as safe as the man defending them, and a man is just as vulnerable as his woman and child make him. Banding together works only as well as there is a stable hierarchy with a good leader at the top. Roy is a good leader."

The brunette. "Or, he was. He might not recover from this."

93

Gray-blond. Confidently. "He'll recover. He has to. He has six dozen adults depending on him. And however many children."

Red head. "What if he doesn't?"

Braids. "Someone will step in. Someone from his inner circle, who's been part of this since the beginning."

They all turned to look at me, and I shrugged, discomfited. "I think he'll recover."

Their skepticism reflected my own worries. I'd finally gotten accustomed to the thought of being part of this House – if it all crumbled, I would be lost again, drowning in uncertainty, or just outright drowning, if a warlord sensed weakness and came in to take over. I shivered, sudden fear welling in my heart. Being stuck here, on the island, was almost as bad as being stuck in a village. I curled around myself, pulling the sheet partially over my face, struggling to keep calm while the other slaves continued to speculate.

Finally exhaustion claimed me.

The next day Jessica's body was laid on a bier and burned. The four outposts took turns sending people in to say good-bye as her spirit mingled with the elements of the world.

People spoke – fragments of memory, dreams come true by her influence. I found myself weeping, and I barely knew her. The ones who did know her were wretched.

When the fire had burned down to the rocky base, water was poured from great jugs, washing the ash down a channel to the river. Roy stood under a weeping willow tree for hours, partially screened by the branches, flanked by the Ward brothers and the two slaves. I found myself wishing I could go to him, wishing I could offer him comfort in any way. But without their request, there wasn't really anything I could do.

The rest of the week the other slaves stayed with us, and I found myself in a position of slight authority – I was most familiar with Lauren, with the way she kept the kitchen and the house, so I offered suggestions when I noticed them doing something she would not approve of.

The first time she caught me doing so, she patted my bottom in passing. "Good little slave mama." I stared at her, confused, until Sara started laughing. She was the slave with braids.

"She means you're taking care of us. Trying to help us stay out of trouble. That's why she called you mama." I frowned, but let it go.

The pat reminded me that I hadn't been spanked in a few days, and my bottom was finally healed up. I rubbed it a bit – nope, not sore. For some reason, it made me miss Jeffrey even more. A thought struck me. Did he even know about Jessica? He'd left before it happened. The more I thought about it, the more I fretted. Him not knowing, him having been her lover – it would be a horrible thing for him to find out, to find out that he'd missed her last day.

It wasn't until the slaves went back to their usual homes elsewhere and things started to settle back to the normal routine of things that Devon took me to his bed again.

His lust sated in my mouth, he'd wrapped his arms around me and kissed my hair. I looked at him curiously. "Why doesn't Jeffery kiss me?"

Devon shrugged. "To him it's too intimate."

I felt like I'd been slapped. "We are very intimate. He wanted to keep me. Why wouldn't he kiss me then?"

Devon shrugged again. "It's his prerogative. Just like it was for him to tell me I could kiss your body, but not your lips."

I frowned at him, but let it go. And the more it bothered me, the more I realized I was starting to care about Jeffery. I decided I would meet Jeffery's boat when it came in.

It struck me that I'd not been allowed out of the house since I'd first arrived. It said something for how preoccupied I was that I hadn't realized it before. Especially given that my whole life up until then had been spent outdoors or close to it. The open shutters had helped. Big windows that looked out on the island and let the breeze in helped me forget. But once I realized it, it was like ripping off a bandage that I hadn't wanted to remove. It ached inside me, the desire to find myself completely in the open air. And it mingled with the desire to meet Jeffery's boat, to tell him what he'd missed before he came into the miserable atmosphere inside the house.

The only problem was that I didn't know what his boat looked like, or when he was coming back. I offered to clean rooms the next day, and Lauren had agreed, a suspicious eye on me. In each room I took in the view from the window, looking for the pier I'd come in on, or any other, for that matter. It wasn't until I found the short flight of stairs set opposite the kitchen that I even found the front door of the house – and sure enough, there was the pier. I stood for a long minute in the doorway, until one of the men patrolling spotted me and came towards me, weapon held as easily in his hands as a rag or cook spoon was in mine. I stood my ground, heart hammering.

"Ma'am? Does the governor need anything?"

I shook my head, my heart in my throat. "No, sir. I'm just airing out the vestibule."

He nodded, and left to continue the circuit he'd been on when he'd detoured. I watched him for a long time, wondering what would happen if I tried to escape. Not that escaping seemed like a smart idea – but I realized how trusting they were of me, when they'd known me for only a few weeks. I was given nearly free range in the house. I wasn't chained to sleep or ever, not since the first day. Had something I'd said or done convinced them I was worthy of that trust?

Devon took me to his bed that night also. This time he lay back, and told me to see if I could make him cum all by myself. I was surprised – not only had I become accustomed to his cock ramming into my throat, but I had come to enjoy it. This was an interesting challenge. So I climbed onto the bed, eager to please.

My touch was tentative, but he just watched my hands with that slow smile. Emboldened, I began to stroke him. His skin was soft and thick, the foreskin slipping easily over the rapidly hardening shaft. I gathered his balls into my palm, rolling them between my fingers. The soft pouch holding his hard stones was fascinating, and it tightened as I played. I tugged some of the hair on it and he jerked.

"Behave, Nanette."

I giggled at his stern expression, and squeezed. He moaned. I grinned. Leaning forward, I extended my tongue and licked just the tip of his cock. He made an impatient sound, so I did it again, barely touching. It was gratifying to see him tense. Dipping my head further, I licked his balls, slowly and thoroughly covering them with layer after layer of saliva. I alternated sucking them into my mouth and warming them, then blowing on them to cool them. His hands clenched into fists in the sheets, and I began to murmur as I sucked, letting the vibration in my throat carry through my tongue to his sensitive spots.

The impatience in his voice made me grin. "Suck my cock, little slave."

So I did, starting at the base and licking slowly – oh so slowly – from the base to the tip. Starting over at the base, I shifted slightly, tracing another line up with my tongue. And again. I coated the underside of his cock with long, slow licks. Wanting more, I sidled around him until my right knee touched the left side of his chest and I could reach the topside of it. Treating it the same with long, slow, tantalizing licks, I licked until he was completely slippery and wet. Then I wrapped my hand around the base of his shaft and started to pump, pulling and squeezing. Sucking the thick head into my mouth, I used my hand to stroke the space between my lips and his pelvis. He groaned behind me, and wrapped an arm around my hips, pulling me closer.

"Suck me deeper."

I complied, taking as much of him into my mouth as I could comfortably fit. He spanked me, and I jumped, my teeth closing.

"No biting!"

He spanked me hard again, and I was careful to keep my tongue between my teeth and his flesh. His fingers found my slick cunt and slid in. I gasped, forcing my head down as far as I could in a thank you.

Holding me steady with one arm, the other pumped slowly inside me, following the speed of my stroking mouth. I moaned, then sped up, and he followed suit. Greedy of pleasure, I bobbed hard on his cock, arching my back to give him better access, groaning as his cock bumped the back of my throat. It was difficult to match the speed I desired in my cunt with the speed I could provide with my head, but I tried. Sucking hard on each backstroke, I tried to stimulate his orgasm. Suddenly, it was successful, and my mouth was filled with cum. I sucked hard, holding my breath until he was finished, then releasing his flesh to swallow. His fingers paused and I whimpered. His breathy chuckle vibrated against my leg. He began to fuck me harder, jamming his fingers in deeper and deeper until the stretch burned and the pressure built up too high. I came, collapsing against him and crying out.

The next morning I asked when Jeffery was coming back.

"Another day or two."

"Does the boat come in the morning?

"Yes, usually. They usually stop at the southernmost outpost for the night before continuing up the river to here."

"Okay." I took a deep breath. "Do you ever want your own slave?"

He finished fastening his overalls and turned to me, running a thumb down my cheek. "Why do you ask, Nanette?"

I blushed. "I don't know. You're one of Roy's closest men. I'm just surprised you don't have one yet."

"I don't want a slave."

I looked up, startled.

He smiled at me. "Don't worry, I enjoy you, little slave."

I flushed.

"But I want a wife. Until then, I'm content to take what Roy and Jeffery allow."

I cocked my head, contemplating him. He didn't seem to have the cruel streak that Jeffery did, nor the overwhelming desire for authority that Roy did. I could see him married – though dominant, of course.

"Now off with you. You want to have good reports for Jeffery when he comes back, don't you?"

I squeaked when he slapped my bottom, sending me into the hallway towards the kitchen.

Lauren sat at the table, her head listing to the side. I immediately went to her, concerned. She eyed me as I sat down and took her hand in mine. "What's wrong, ma'am? Is there anything I can do to help you?"

She shook her head. "No, girl. I'm just exhausted."

I frowned. She always seemed so strong, like nothing could get her down. The men started to filter into the dining room, and I watched her make an effort to pull herself together. I realized she must have known Jessica for a long time too, but she'd spent all her energy on helping keep the rest of the House fed and the building clean. Not a single time in the last week had I seen her take a break for herself.

I looked around. There was the pot for the porridge, but it wasn't even started yet. The men needed to eat before they went to work. I stood up. Putting on my best stern face, I shook my finger at her. "You sit there. I'll cook."

I had learned basic cooking from my mother, and felt a pang of longing, but I ignored it. Quickly, I scooped in enough of the dry rice, heating the pan on the flat metal burner. Stirring it until it was toasty, I struggled with the big water jug, but managed to get the water in. At least, I hoped it was enough. I could always add more later if I needed to. Stirring it and then putting a lid on, I pulled out bowls from the cabinet. Checking who was in the dining room, I set them on the worktable and started pulling down jars of fruits and vegetables. "What does Tobin eat on his?"

She watched me bustle around, bemused. "No fruit. All nuts, chopped fine, a drizzle of honey." I chopped the nuts and scooped them into a smaller bowl. It would mean more washing later, but if I could get the toppings ready while the porridge cooked, it would take less time to get it on the table for their breakfast.

"How about Gerard?" Around we went, as I prepared the

toppings in between stirs of the rice. There were only a few men there that I didn't recognize, but Lauren knew them all by sight, knew their food preferences like the back of her hand. I marveled at the knowledge she'd stored up.

Eventually, one of the men came up to the counter to inquire about the food. "Lauren? How's it coming?"

Before she could answer I jumped in. "I have to do it all today. I have to prove I can cook breakfast all by myself." I looked up at him with wide eyes. "I'm so sorry it's running late." He blinked at me, and glanced to Lauren, who'd managed to sit up straight and look as indomitable as she usually did.

"It'll be out shortly, Ian."

He went back to his seat and I returned to chopping the dried fruit for his porridge. She watched me, an unreadable look on her face. "What was the purpose of that?"

I glanced up at her. "I didn't think you wanted anyone to see you in a moment of weakness."

She didn't answer, and I stirred the porridge again. It looked done, so I tasted a bit. Good enough. I carried the heavy pot to the table and started ladling it out, then dumping the toppings on. Sticking spoons in, I carried them out to the table. Ian made sure to compliment me, so I grinned at him.

I put Lauren's bowl in front of her. "Eat, please, ma'am. Then tell me what the essential things are to do today."

She reached for the bowl, and took a bite. "Not enough honey." I picked up the honey jar and poured another dollop onto her bowl, more than I knew she wanted. She caught my eye and I smiled. I was definitely finding my place in this House.

When the men were finished eating, I collected their bowls and wished them good day. Roy remained where he was, slumped in his chair. Tobin stood nearby, Stephanie at his feet. Her eyes were swollen and red, her posture defeated. I went to Roy, unsure if I should try to speak to him or not.

"My lord?"

Stephanie looked up, her eyes narrowing as she considered something. I edged further away from her, wary.

"My lord, is there anything I can get you?"

Stephanie leaned closer. I bit my lip. Feeling very much like a rabbit right before a snake strike, I shifted a half step away. She stood up.

"Stephanie..." Tobin's voice held a warning note that she completely ignored. One foot shifted forward, and then she slapped me, full across the face, sending me sprawling. I looked up from the floor, shocked, as she leaned over and spit venom.

"No! There's nothing at all you can get for him. Nothing at all you can get for any of us. You didn't know her. You didn't care. You're nothing. You're just a worthless, miserable bit of slave that was good for nothing more than warming Jeffery's bed for a few nights. I bet he's forgotten all about you in his nights with the whores in the village!" Her voice had risen as she spoke, and by the end she was struggling furiously in Tobin's iron grip. Roy looked up, his eyes full of anger.

"How *dare* you speak to her that way. Nanette has been nothing but kind and well behaved. Unlike some little bitches I know." He stood up to his full height, something I hadn't seen him do since Jessica passed. Her eyes got big and her struggling ceased immediately.

"Please. My lord. Please. Have mercy."

He ignored her, helping me up instead. "Nanette, go to the kitchen and let Lauren have a look at that."

I whimpered, feeling wet on my cheek. He dropped a kiss on my head along with a hug.

"You're a good girl. It's not your fault you didn't know Jessica better. You've proven yourself to be a valuable asset to this house."

I nodded, eyes filled with tears, and he turned me with a gentle shove towards the kitchen. He grabbed Stephanie's hair and shoved her forward until she stumbled, landing on her knees on the hard floor. A quick glance over her shoulder abruptly let me know she was concerned for me.

"Please!"

He thundered at her. "GO!" She scrambled forward in the direction of the dungeon. Tobin followed, and Roy after. I hid in the kitchen, shaking. Lauren was already there with clean cloths and antiseptic.

"You'll be fine. It's not a big cut."

I flinched at the stinging dab.

"She did it on purpose."

Lauren looked up. "You caught that? Yes, she did."

"Why? Why would she want to make him so angry?"

"She wanted to pull him out of his misery. Anger goads him into motion. Whipping her will give him a chance to clear his thoughts, to work out some of the dark emotions he has. It will remind him he has a duty to her and the rest of his people."

"But she sounded really scared."

Lauren snorted. "If she wasn't afraid she'd be stupid. She's getting a very harsh punishment right now." As if on cue, a wailing scream came from the dungeon. "She earned it. Roy doesn't punish without cause – so she had to earn it. And if she did, well, she'll take it."

A grudging admiration found room in my heart for her. I couldn't behave like she did – not in a thousand years – but I admired her determination to help her master, no matter what the cost to her own skin. The screams continued and I shivered. "He won't – won't harm her, will he?"

"No. Tobin is there, too – Tobin loves her more than anything in this world, just like Roy loved Jessica. Roy loves Stephanie, too. They've been together a very long time – Roy knows what he's doing. He won't harm her."

I nodded, not completely convinced.

Lauren sat down, heaving a sigh. "You still up to helping me today?"

"Of course." I took a deep breath, putting Stephanie's words behind me. It helped, knowing that they were a deliberate provocation, meant to trigger the greatest anger she could, but it ate at me, not knowing when Jeffery was going to be back, or if he really had that little concern for me. I didn't think it was true. I hoped it wasn't true. Not when I was starting to care for him.

The day passed slowly. I'd become accustomed to working with Lauren, but hadn't realized quite how much she did on her own until I tried to do it. All the while, I scolded and nagged, making sure she rested and relaxed as much as she could. I needed this House to stay stable, both for my own well being and Suzanna's, and for the rest of the people who belonged to Roy.

After supper, I tucked Lauren into bed and promised to finish cleaning the kitchen myself. It wore on me, scrubbing and wiping and putting everything away when I was already past exhaustion. Finally it was over. I turned to see Devon watching me in the gloom.

"Yes, sir?"

"Come to bed, Nanette."

I followed him down the hall. In the room, he had a tub ready. "Get in."

I obeyed. "Thank you, sir."

He took the cloth and washed me, his hard hands digging into the sore muscles of my back and shoulders. It hurt, but it also rubbed out the tension.

"Roy told me what Stephanie said."

I flushed and looked down.

"He also told me what you did this morning, how you've been helping Lauren all day."

I glanced up. He'd noticed all that? "Sir?"

"I don't know if my brother loves you yet, or if he ever will. But know that you are valuable, and appreciated here. Know that I am grateful you stumbled across our net with Suzanna."

I looked up at him, and saw a measure of care in his eyes he hadn't let me see before. Gently, he leaned down and kissed the tip of my nose, smiling as he drew back. I watched him, my heart stirring with unaccustomed emotions. He finished my bath, then washed himself quickly while I dried. In bed, he tucked me against his chest, his lips against my hair.

"Sleep, little slave."

CHAPTER
TEN

I WOKE AT DAWN. Devon was gone. I pulled on a clean dress and slipped quickly down the hall to the front door. There he was, walking towards the pier – and there was a great boat pulling in. My heart burst at the sight of Jeffery, standing tall and broad in the middle. Without thinking, I ran towards him.

The grass was prickly under feet softened by weeks of smooth floors, the dress flying about my legs immodestly. I stopped short, skidding a little on the wet boards of the long pier when I caught sight of his face. He knew. He knew already – of course he did. We were still wearing white – he would have known as soon as he came close, as soon as he saw Devon. His face was dark, and he didn't acknowledge me or his brother, merely continued giving orders for the docking. When the boat was secured, and the unloading had begun – it looked like the House traded brined fish for what staples we couldn't grow or make ourselves – he jumped down. Embracing his brother in a fierce hug, they pounded each other's backs, and then I saw tears. Both of them were crying, no shame, merely two men mourning the loss of a beloved woman. I stood awkward, skittering back out of the way of the other men when they needed the room to continue unloading. Jeffery had a new mark on his arm, a stylistic woman's profile with what looked like a name written on it. I bit my lip. If I had to guess, it was Jessica's name.

Swallowing hard, all of Stephanie's angry words came back in my head. Maybe he hadn't spent the week with whores. Maybe he had spent it mourning his lover. Maybe I really was nothing but a pale substitute for her luminescence. I turned away, starting to run – down the shore, away from the house.

I stumbled, slipping down the incline until I was knee-deep in the water, scrambling for purchase, and then a hard grip caught my arm, hauling me up. Jeffery's eyes searched my own.

"Are you trying to escape?"

I shook my head frantically, off balance in his grasp. He shook me.

"Do you want to be crocodile bait? What the hell were you running that close to the edge for?"

"I'm sorry!"

He shook me again. "You will be." His voice was grim and I struggled, twisting as he marched me up to the house, back in through the door.

"Please! Jeffery! I'll be good! I wasn't trying to run away, honest! I wasn't trying to go in the water! Really! Please!"

"You'll be even better once you get a hard spanking, little slave."

I whimpered, stumbling along beside him as he led me down the hall, into the dungeon. "Tobin?" No answer. I looked past him, and Stephanie was chained to one of the long benches, face down, her naked body covered in crimson welts from her shoulders to her calves. I bit back a cry of dismay. She seemed to be sleeping. He ignored her then, and shoved me over one of the strange benches. Tucking my knees onto the smaller cushion, he chained them down and I cried out.

"Please! Please! Please! I'm sorry!"

"You'll be more sorry in a minute."

I slapped at his hands when he tried to chain my forearms, but he smacked my hands and chained them anyway, my elbows resting on the small cushion on the other side, my hips pressed into the bigger middle cushion.

Standing in front of me he grasped the knots of fabric on my shoulders and jerked, the wet fabric scraping over my nipples as it came off. I cried out, my breasts flopping loose past the edge of the cushion. He stalked around behind me.

"No wonder you're such a naughty slave today. My brother hasn't disciplined you at all." His hand caressed my bare bottom roughly, prodding and squeezing as he determined I hadn't been really spanked since he'd left.

I tried one more time. "That's because I've been *good!*"

He growled. "Just because you've been good for a few days doesn't mean you don't need your ass walloped now." The words sent a spike of fear and arousal through my chest that settled down along my belly and my cunt. I gasped.

"No, please, Jeffery!"

Silence. I realized my mistake. "I'm sorry! Sir! Please, sir!" The first splat of his hand on my ass astounded me. The next, and the next and the next, fast and furious, built up until I sucked in air and wailed. He pressed a hand into the small of my back, putting pressure on the chain belt. I whimpered, then wailed again as his hand cracked down the backs of my thighs. Drumming my shins frantically, I tried to escape, to reposition, to do anything other than present my body for his punishment.

"Defiance? I can definitely see you need a hard spanking."

"No, sir, please!"

"Yes, little slave. You need to be kept sore, to remember who your master is."

"Please, sir!"

"You don't run away from me. Not ever, Nanette."

"No, sir, I won't, I won't, never again!"

"I expect you won't." His hand slapped down on my upturned bottom, burning my skin. He started at the top of my crack, spanking hard and fast until I was frantic. When he was satisfied that my skin was on fire, his hand shifted down and he continued spanking, his calloused fingers raising welts. I felt tears splash down on my arms and I tossed my head, struggling for air, but it was no use. I was bound down securely. The padded top pressed my belly so I couldn't wiggle forward – the only direction I could possibly move was backwards, towards his punishing hand. And I absolutely did not want to do that.

His hand shifted lower, cracking down again and again across the fullest part of my bottom. My cries dissolved into one drawn out wail, and I shuddered, the heat branding my bottom. I wondered if I would be able to sit down ever again. I wondered if he was going to spank me until he wore himself out, and if my ass would give out before then. I wondered what Stephanie thought of my punishment, and if it pleased her. I wondered why Jeffery was so angry with me.

His hand shifted lower, and suddenly it was branding my sweet spot, the tender crease between buttock and thigh. I howled. After a long time, when I had completely lost track of the number of spanks he applied, he stopped. I gasped in relief, my breath hitching with sobs.

"You are going to stay with me, aren't you, Nanette?"

"Yes, sir! Yes, sir!"

"You will be careful, and not risk yourself on the shore, won't you?"

"Yes, sir! Yes, sir!"

He spanked my sweet spot again, his hand reinforcing his words. "You'll be a good little slave, with your bottom sore, won't you?"

It was difficult to answer around my tears, but I managed. "Y-yes, s-sir! Y-y-yes, s-s-sir!"

"Good girl, Nanette. Good little slave."

I finally gave in, my body limp over the padded bench, unable to resist his harsh discipline. His spanking hand shifted to my thighs, and I struggled, but the flare of defiance was short-lived. I moaned, tears flowing freely, snot dripping from my nose, as he burned my thighs crimson.

I lost track of anything except pain. Time seemed suspended, a sort of not quite there space where I reacted to each explosion of pain, but had no thoughts beyond it. All I wanted was to submit to Jeffery, to obey him, to please him.

My body reacted. Burning heat wrapped itself inside my core, and I ripened, aching for his ungentle tenderness. My thighs spread as far as possible in the chains, opening my naked body to his view. I pressed back towards his harsh hand, begging for his discipline.

"Please. Sir. Please." I didn't understand why my voice was soft, or why I wasn't asking him to stop anymore. I just knew I belonged to him, more than any other person in the world, and I wanted him to know I understood. "Please."

His hand stilled, and he stroked my welted skin. "You are a good girl, aren't you, Nanette?"

"Yes. Sir." My voice was low, crooning the answers.

"You belong to me, don't you?"

"Yes. Sir."

"You are my slave."

"Yes. Sir."

"Good." His hands, when they unfastened the chains, were exceptionally gentle. I stayed where I was, tears dripping on my chain-marked forearms. He lifted me to stand, and I slid down to my knees, my head falling back as I tried to look up at him.

"Sir."

He caressed my face, and then lifted me again, carrying me to his room. He laid me on the bed, and I cried out at the touch of the sheets on my backside. He spread my thighs, and let my legs fall apart, limp.

"Yes."

He removed his clothes, and I watched him, admiring the sheen of sweat across his hard chest, the play of his muscles under his tanned skin. I moaned with pleasure as his cock sprang free of his pants and he knelt on the bed between my thighs.

"Please." My murmur was almost a prayer.

"Such a good little slave." He slipped his cock inside my cunt for the first time, sliding in deep until I was completely filled.

"Yes!" I arched my hips against him, wanting more, always more. He leaned on his elbows, and his lips brushed mine. I ached for him. My whole body throbbed with want. He brushed my lips again, and then crushed them beneath his, biting and thrusting with his tongue until I had no other thoughts beyond overwhelming joy. I kissed him back, my own tongue dueling with his, my hands tangling in his hair of their own accord. He thrust his hips against mine. I moaned, my whole body opening up to him, vulnerable.

I wrapped my legs around his hips, and he released my mouth long enough to grin that cruel grin at me. "Keep your legs there, or I'll spank your tits, too."

I tried. I really did. But his fucking was harsh and wild, and eventually I lost my grip on his hips. He knelt up, and I moaned, desiring and terrified. His hands were gentler on my breasts than my buttocks, but they still stung fiercely. He spanked the sides of my breasts, causing them to flop together. When my hands got in the way he tucked them behind my head, nipping my ear as he did so. His hands came down on the top of my tits, then he spanked the inner sides. All the while, his cock was buried inside me, reminding me to whom I belonged.

Finally, he grasped a nipple and lifted it, spanking the underside of my tit so hard I squirmed and cried, the throbbing pain sending lightning bolts to my clit. I groaned, arching my back up towards his hands. He obliged, grasping my other nipple and spanking hard on the underside of that tit. When he was satisfied with the burn in my ample flesh, he began to spank my nipples. I wailed, my hands in the way again. He leaned in, his voice harsh in my ear. "Grab my shoulders, and hold on. If you block my hands again, I'll spank them twice as much."

I whimpered, nodding, and wrapped my hands around his shoulders. He continued to spank my nipples, the hard buds radiating pain.

When he was satisfied with the color of my well-punished tits, he leaned down and pressed them together, sucking the tips into his mouth. I screamed again, this time in pleasure. His pelvis slammed into mine and I wrapped my legs around him again, then hung on as I was tossed against the bed like a boat on a stormy sea. The waves that crashed into my body flipped me under until I was drowned in pleasure. He didn't stop fucking me, only increased the intensity. His lips found mine again, and I screamed when I came. He continued, driving me off the cliff another two times before he orgasmed inside me.

I lay limp, completely worn out. He pressed little kisses down the side of my jaw, the side of my neck, his tongue flicking the padlock. I moaned softly, content to lay under him forever.

When I came to again his weight was still pinning me to the bed, and I hummed under my breath. His deep breathing fanned across my neck and his arms were relaxed, holding me close. My hips ached with being forced so wide for so long, so I wiggled under him. He didn't move. I wiggled some more, but he was a lead weight. I shifted over and pressed my lips to his, pleased to see his eyes flutter open. I smiled at him.

"Good little slave." He kissed me then, bruising my lips until I moaned. He shifted, lifting off me and flipping me over. He tucked my knees together, raising my throbbing ass high and shoving my face down. "Spread your ass cheeks for me." I flushed red, then reached back and did as he said, giving him access to my bottom hole. He dipped fingers into my sopping cunt and painted my crack, then pressed the blunt head of his cock against it. "Relax, little slave."

I concentrated on opening my tight hole, and his thick cock slipped in. I gasped, clenching at the still unfamiliar sensation. He slid out, and then slammed deep inside. I moaned, the sensations increasing with each thrust until I was a mewling bundle of aching needs. His hips banged my sore bottom, his hairy legs tormenting my welted thighs. That spot inside that brought me the greatest pleasure was rubbed with every thrust, and I began to cry out. His hands on my hips steadied me, grounded me, even as he pounded my ass until I lost myself in spasms of pleasure. His seed erupted, burning me from the inside with each hot spurt.

We slept again. When I awoke, we were on our sides, his limbs tangled around mine. I wiggled closer, comforted by the beat of his heart, the tenderness in his hands.

Devon came in the room, and sat on the edge of the bed closest to me, reaching a calloused hand out to caress my face. "You see." His smile was warm and happy. "You see he cares about you a great deal."

I nodded, rubbing my cheek against his palm.

"When you get up, he needs to come out to the dock. There are questions for him, but he left abruptly." His amusement seemed to show there was no anger at Jeffery, so I didn't feel I had to wake him immediately. Instead, I settled against him, breathing deeply. Devon kissed my cheek and exited. I lay still, savoring the lazy calm. My bottom throbbed and ached, as did my insides, but I felt safe, like I belonged here. Here, on this island, as a part of this House. Here, in Jeffery's arms and in his bed. I drifted.

I focused on the noise in the room. Stephanie was there, directing the men carrying a tub. She knelt beside the bed, and I frowned at her.

Her voice was hoarse. "I'm sorry."

"For what?"

"For giving you doubts. For getting you in trouble."

I reached a finger to her swollen face, mottled with crying. Her skin was soft and I reveled in it, stroking the wisps of hair between my fingers. It was like satin. I pushed myself up on an elbow.

"You didn't get me in trouble. I ran from Jeffery."

She managed a smile. "Foolish little slave."

Jeffery reached out from behind me, grasping her chin. "Ah. Still a brat, aren't you?"

She stared at him, one eyebrow raised in disdain. It didn't seem to bother him. He patted her cheek, just hard enough to move her head. "Be a good girl and wash us off."

Face flushed with humiliation, she obeyed. It was painful to sit in the tub with my buttocks as swollen as they were, but Jeffery pulled me into his lap. He washed me, and Stephanie washed him. I think he found it amusing to watch her have to bite her tongue and behave for once.

When we were clean and dressed in fresh clothes, he took my

hand, leading me outside. He stopped at the door and laced on thick leather boots – I was offered nothing. So when the grass poked my feet, I kept quiet, but looked for rocks, shells or other sharp objects to avoid.

"Jeffery! I have questions for you." The big man waving from the dock caught Jeffery's attention and he went. I followed slowly, hanging back from the water, watching the men work. Contentment threaded its way through my thoughts as I considered the direction my life had taken. I belonged to this house with a certainty I hadn't felt since I belonged to my parents' house. And with them gone – dead or lost, who could say? – I needed another anchor. I needed a safe place to live. And here – I was protected from the outside world, and protected from myself. My bottom throbbed, and I placed my palms flat on it, feeling the heat that radiated through the fabric of my dress.

The sun beat down on us, reflecting off the water and dazzling my eyes. My skin warmed further while a breeze teased the cloth that covered me. I tasted the tang of the river in the air, breathing in the scent of fish, and tomatoes from the huge garden off to the side. I could hear gulls calling as they milled around above us. Still, my attention remained focused on Jeffery.

His cruel streak endeared me to him. My sore cunt ached with the pleasure he brought me. The welts and raw spots on my buttocks and thighs were a small price to pay for the contentment that having a home and a hierarchy brought me.

Could I raise a child here? If his seed took root inside me? I tipped my head up to the sun, and called her name. *Eris? I think I could. I think I could have a child here.*

It was not to be. Not yet.

It was midday before he finished working, and by then I'd shifted to kneeling on the grass, grateful for the rest from house and kitchen duties, a vague guilt stirring that I hadn't offered to go back and help. A bee buzzed by quietly, and I drowsed, a steady heat in my core at the sight of his brawn, lifting and hauling crates, his commanding stance as he directed the actions of the other men.

When it was dinnertime, he directed them all towards the house. I stood up as he approached me. Wrapping his arms around my waist, he tucked me close and kissed me hard.

"I've been wanting to do that for a long time."

I leaned on his shoulder. "Why wait?"

He smiled down at me. "I only kiss those who are important to me."

I pouted. "So I wasn't important until today?"

He put his lips by my ear and whispered until I squirmed. "Of course you were. But I wanted to wait and be sure that my intuition about your importance wasn't wrong."

"Oh?"

"I wanted to kiss you the first day I saw you."

I blushed, my face buried against his chest. "Oh."

"But now I have the rest of your life to kiss you."

"Oh." I thought about it. Would I ever leave him? In my entire life? Hard to say. But I didn't think so.

"We missed breakfast. We should go have dinner." He took my smaller hand in his big one and led me back to the house. Pausing to remove his boots, he swept me into the house and I giggled.

There the men were, milling and talking, while Lauren worked as quickly as she could, two slaves helping out. A quick pat on my bottom from my master and I was in the thick of it, passing ingredients and stirring pots.

"Oh, good, you're back. Chop this ham."

"Yes, ma'am."

After dinner was served, Jeffery snapped his fingers, and I found myself kneeling on the cushion by his feet. His fingers tangled in my hair and I sighed, my cheek resting on his leg. He put my plate on the floor, and I leaned over, eating at my master's whim. Meandering contentment wound its way through my heart and I pressed close to his calf, eager to touch any part of him I could reach.

After dinner he left the building to work with the fishermen, and I was led to his room by Jacqueline. My pack was there.

I looked askance at her. "What? Why?"

"We had to be sure you were ready to stay. But as long as you do stay, you may do whatever you wish with your belongings." I knelt down, touching the dirty fabric. It was all I had left of my former home, the reminder like a splash of cold water on my face. I opened it and began to remove things. The fish was already gone, and I was grateful that someone had searched the pack already – that poor fish would be a rotten mess by now if they hadn't. There was the net, and my blanket, and the mosquito net, the pots and pans, flint and steel, the fishing line and hooks, the bag of coins, my binoculars, the change of clothing.

"May I put these things in the laundry?"

She nodded. I piled them into three categories, then collected all the fabric, including the dirty pack, and tossed them into the hamper. As I did, something clunked. I checked all the pockets again, and there it was, tucked in the corner fold of one where I hadn't noticed it before. One of the rings my mother used to wear, up until the day we left. I was right – she wasn't wearing them when they woke us up. She must have put it there when packing the bag. I wiped it with the hem of my dress and slipped it on my finger. It fit. I remembered her voice, when I was younger. *This one is yours, Nanette. When you're older.* It was mine now. And somehow, knowing that she didn't believe she would see me again dropped a stone in my heart. Mourning, I kissed it, my eyes closing against the tears that wouldn't come. For a long time I stayed, reliving my favorite memories of her. I didn't know how much time passed, but Jacqueline waited, somehow sensing my grief.

When I could face the world again, I placed the coins and tools on the top of my master's wooden chest, and gathered the pots and pans and jugs. These, I took to the kitchen.

"What is that?"

"My pots and pans from home. When the sink is free, I'd like to wash them."

Lauren nodded.

"And this is the last of my vinegar, and the last of my salt."

She took them carefully, and set them down on the counter.

"Thank you." I spent the afternoon helping Lauren, and when there was a lull, I washed my things, putting them in a corner of the shelf, out of the way.

There was a bit of a commotion right before supper. A young woman had trespassed on our territory. She had a child with her, a little one not much more than a baby, strapped to a sling on her back. I went to the window with the other slaves, watching as the boat with her pulled in. She seemed to have been aiming for our territory, however, as she didn't struggle against the hands that held her, lifting her out of the boat.

Lauren turned to the redhead beside me. "Fiona, get Marcus. And Nanette, get Ian." Fiona raced off down the island. I turned to the dining room and found Ian, leading him to the vestibule where the men had brought her. I could see she was dirty and frightened, but thankful to have arrived. I watched the men around her – they were standing protectively. She wasn't in danger. Roy entered the room, and they made way for him. She sank to her knees, rocking and petting the child she carried close to her chest.

"I hear you asked for my protection."

"Yes, governor."

"What is your name?"

"Katarina, sir."

"Welcome, Katarina." He looked around, spotting Ian when I shoved him forward a step. If Lauren wanted him there, there was a reason. "Ian. You have room in your house. Will you take her in, take responsibility for her?"

"Yes, sir." He looked back at the woman, her breathing rapid with fear. Marcus came in through the front door, Suzanna trailing him, one of his daughters and Julia coming behind. Suzanna knelt in front of Katarina.

"It's okay. We'll take good care of you. Can Julia take a look at your baby?"

The young woman glanced at Julia, and back to Suzanna. My sister held out her hands, and reluctantly, she lifted the child out of the sling. Suzanna passed the child to Julia, who checked her over carefully. Marcus helped Katarina stand, and looked her over as non-intrusively as he could.

"Nothing a hot bath and a week of good meals won't cure."

Roy nodded. "Ian, see to it. You are excused for the rest of the day."

With a quick nod, Ian took her elbow, and Julia passed the fussing child back. They left through the front door, and gradually, the rest of the men dispersed. A couple followed Roy, and I assumed they were going to report to him on where they'd found Katarina. Suzanna stood awkwardly in the vestibule as Marcus and Julia spoke in low tones. I went to her, hugging her hard, tugging her a little ways away so we could speak without being overheard. It wasn't until after I'd released her that I realized she had a ring on her finger. It was our mother's other ring, the one that had been promised to Suzanna.

Tears finally broke free and slid down my face when I saw it. "You found it."

"You found the other one."

We stared at each other's rings. I wondered how long Mom had known we would have to run, wondered how much it hurt her to send her daughters off into the wilderness alone, and it broke my heart. We clung to each other for a long time. I thought about Daddy, and how hopeless it must have been, if he didn't think he could protect us any more, if he had to trust to fate to see us through.

Fate, and his eldest daughter. I hadn't gotten to where he intended us to go, but I had gotten us somewhere safe. Somewhere I could see us living for a long time. I set Suzanna back from me, searching her face.

"How are you with Marcus and Julia? Are they good to you? How about the other daughters?"

"They're fine. I'm good. They've been really nice to me. I got my stuff back yesterday, and Julia is altering some of my clothes for here."

"That's very nice of her."

"Yeah, it is."

"I – Suzanna, I don't know how to say this, but, I want to stay here. I want to stay with Jeffery."

"Really?" She searched my eyes, looking for any hint of coercion, any sign of abuse. "Are you sure?"

"I'm as sure as I can be. We need this kind of stability."

She heaved a sigh, and I worried. "Do you want to leave? If something's wrong, you need to tell me, Suzanna." I grabbed her hands, pleading with her. Maybe I hadn't done as well as I thought?

She shook her head, half-laughing. "No, that's not it. I'm just relieved. I – I feel like I've found a place that I can learn to call home. And when Mom and Daddy find us, maybe it will be different. But for now – I don't want to leave. I was just afraid you would – that Jeffery would hurt you and you wouldn't want to stay."

I smiled at her, gathering her into my embrace again. "I'm fine. I love you. Don't worry – let's stay. As long as we're both safe here."

She smiled at me. "Did you know how many cute guys live at the other end of the island?"

I smacked her shoulder, aghast. "You behave yourself, Suzanna! You're only twelve."

She narrowed her eyes at me. "I told them the truth the other day. So you can stop pretending."

I relented, still wishing I could slow down time, hold back the day she'd have to choose to marry or become a slave.

"I'm fourteen and I have eyes."

I rolled mine. Typical teenager. "Fine. Just – please, Suzanna, stay out of trouble."

"Oh, like you do?"

She poked me, and I suddenly wondered how many people had seen my mad dash along the shore, had known exactly how much trouble I was in this morning. I blushed. "That's different."

She raised an eyebrow, looking so much like Daddy for a minute it made a lump in my throat. "For now."

I agreed. "For now."

Roy came back into the vestibule then, looking for Marcus and Julia. He patted Suzanna on the head like a small child, and spanked me hard on my sore bottom, eliciting a yelp. "Get back to where you're supposed to be."

I turned to obey immediately. "Yes, sir."

CERISE NOBLE

Cerise Noble is a storyteller. Her stories range from written books (like this one!) to onstage kinky performances (sexy!) to the delightful noises she makes when playing with people she enjoys (at least, people tell her they're delightful – but maybe they're just trying to get into her pants... oh wait, she wasn't wearing any by then...).

Speaking of people she enjoys, there's the Owner with his paddles (wood hurts! Ow!), the BFF who's a witch (can we say "magical"?), the Minx with a pair of floggers (Florentine!), and the rest of the lovelies she plays with on a regular or non-regular basis. Want to play with her? Fetlife is your friend!

When not playing, she enjoys dark chocolate, cranberry anything, her bandana, a bottle of water... wait, that's her list for aftercare. Well, that's good to know, too! Let's see – reading, writing and arithmetic... mmm, poly-math and more-somes... Wait, what were we talking about again?

Don't miss these exciting titles by Cerise Noble!

Brackish Bay Series

Nanette's Capture

121

Stephanie's Slavery
Jacqueline's Disgrace
Jacqueline's Pleasure
Marri's Struggle
Marri's Conflicts
Marri's Approach

Standalone Titles

His Three Wives
Lellen's Journey
Bianka's Baby

Reader's favorite romance eBook publisher of sweet, spicy and sizzling hot romance novels. The best deals on steamy romance books: sexy cowboys, protective alpha males, dangerous mafia men, MC motorcycle club romance and more. Your new book boyfriend crush is just page away. For over over 20 years, Romance Ink has published the hottest taboo and edgy romance books around.

https://www.romance.ink/